"Don't worry, I'm not going to force you."

"I didn't think you would," Claire managed to say.

"Really? Claire, why don't you want to see me?"

Because I don't want to be alone with you. Because you wouldn't have to force me. All you'd have to do is touch me and I'd fall at your feet. "Because there's no reason to see you."

"I disagree. Whether you acknowledge it or not, there's something between us."

"Yes," she admitted, "there *is*. We share a child."

"Who proves we were once in love," he said.

"The key word is 'once,' Jack," she told him. "I tried to make that clear to you. The only reason I'm here is because of our daughter. What do you want from me?"

"I want the truth."

Dear Reader,

When two people fall in love, the world is suddenly new and exciting, and it's that same excitement we bring to you in Silhouette Intimate Moments. These are stories with scope and grandeur. The characters lead lives we all dream of, and everything they do reflects the wonder of being in love.

Longer and more sensuous than most romances, Silhouette Intimate Moments novels take you away from everyday life and let you share the magic of love. Adventure, glamour, drama, even suspense— these are the passwords that let you into a world where love has a power beyond the ordinary, where the best authors in the field today create stories of love and commitment that will stay with you always.

In coming months look for novels by your favorite authors: Kathleen Eagle, Heather Graham Pozzessere, Nora Roberts and Marilyn Pappano, to name just a few. And whenever you buy books, look for all the Silhouette Intimate Moments, love stories *for* today's woman *by* today's woman.

Leslie J. Wainger
Senior Editor
Silhouette Books

Jan Milella
Once Forgotten

Silhouette Intimate Moments

Published by Silhouette Books New York

America's Publisher of Contemporary Romance

SILHOUETTE BOOKS
300 East 42nd St., New York, N.Y. 10017

ISBN: 0-373-07269-4

First Silhouette Books printing January 1989

Printed in the U.S.A.

Books by Jan Milella

Silhouette Intimate Moments

Night Heat #175
Once Forgotten #269

JAN MILELLA

is from Kentucky but considers herself a transplanted Yankee and has called Chicago home for most of her life. In addition to being an author, Jan is a wife, mother, volunteer, registered nurse and unregistered chauffeur—not necessarily in that order. She has been published under the pseudonyms of Jan Mathews and Jan Michaels.

Chapter 1

Claire Brady glanced out the window of the medical evacuation plane carrying her and her daughter from Los Angeles to Minneapolis, Minnesota. As the jet taxied toward a hangar, a brisk wind blew snow in swirling puffs across the cold, frozen runway. A winter storm had shut down the airport last night, but they were able to land now that it was early morning. They had flown into the dawn, and the day was bright and new and pristine white. In the distance Claire could see the helicopter waiting to take her and her child on the last leg of their journey to the kidney unit at County General Hospital.

Meghan's only chance.

She turned toward the little girl lying so still and silent on the white-shrouded hospital cart, her dark hair spilling out across the pillow. Her daughter was so tiny. So fragile. So desperately ill. Claire sighed as she ran a hand through her own dusty blond hair, sweeping the strands back from her face. Unfortunately Meghan's only chance was going to be Claire's agony. She had dreaded this trip, and not only because she had a sick child, although hearing Meghan's diagnosis last night had nearly destroyed her. All she needed now was hope and courage and a miracle or two. And Jack. How she needed Jack.

She could see him waiting near the hangar, his blue down coat open to the elements and his dark hair blowing in the gusts from the powerful rotors. He looked the same as he had when they'd first met five years ago: tall and darkly handsome. Strong. Capable. Someone to lean on.

"Looks like we're here," the doctor who had accompanied her and Meghan from Los Angeles remarked as the plane continued to taxi toward the helicopter.

"Yes," Claire answered. "Yes, it does."

"I see Dr. Brady is waiting."

Claire nodded. "He planned to meet us here."

She doubted she could have kept him away. Late last night, when she'd called him, he had been stunned by Meghan's diagnosis, almost as stunned as she had been when the doctors had given her the news an hour earlier. Acute nephritis. Kidney disease. Their child was gravely ill. She might not survive.

At first Claire had felt as though her head were in some cloud, far away in another universe. This wasn't happening to her. Meghan wasn't sick. She wasn't going to have to see Jack again, go through the pain, dredge up the memories of their ill-fated marriage. Everything was fine.

But everything wasn't fine, she'd realized moments later, and immediately she'd called him, knowing instinctively that he would help. Despite the divorce, despite the bitterness, despite their problems, Jack would help her. He would know what to do.

She hadn't even bothered to try to reach him at his apartment. Although it had been late at night, she'd found him at his unit, exactly where she'd expected he would be. Even before they had split up, he had devoted his life to medicine and to County General Hospital. After his momentary panic—strange, he seldom let down his guard, but even over the phone she had felt his pain, his vulnerability—he had assured her that he would make the arrangements to transfer Meghan to his kidney unit immediately. The plane had arrived practically the second she'd hung up the telephone.

Claire glanced at her watch. It was only nine in the morning, seven her time. Meghan was still asleep. After the initial excitement of an airplane ride and the prospect of seeing her father, exhaustion from her illness had overwhelmed the child and she had drifted off, clutching a ragtag teddy bear in her arms. Claire had given her the teddy bear that first Christmas they'd been alone.

The little girl looked exactly like Jack. They had the same dark, Italian visage and blue Irish eyes and stubborn chin. Only now, her daughter's complexion was pasty, almost yellow. She seemed frail and weak. An intravenuous solution dripped slowly into her arm. Claire leaned forward. "Shall I wake her?"

"Not just yet," the doctor answered. "It'll be a few more minutes until we're ready to transfer her to the helicopter. You're lucky to be going to County General," he went on, bundling up his supplies. "It's a great hospital and they have a wonderful kidney unit."

"Yes, I know." Claire nodded.

"And unquestionably Dr. Brady is the best kidney specialist in the world." He frowned. "Would you be . . . Are you related to Dr. Brady?"

Claire glanced at him. Most of the night he'd kept busy with Meghan, fussing with this and that while Claire had pretended to sleep. "Why do you ask?"

He shrugged. "I just wondered. He's a very famous man."

That was something Claire didn't have to be told. If there was anyone who could help Meghan, it would be Jack. When Claire had met him he had been a young resident; now he was a prominent physician. When he had first opened his unit, he had appeared on television talk shows and had been quoted in all the papers, had been credited with saving many lives. He still saved lives, although the publicity had died down, to be replaced by another headline, another medical entity: a new and different technique of transplant surgery. As Meghan's father, he couldn't be the physician of record, but he could be a consultant on her case. He had worked miracles with others, and Meghan would have the benefit of his knowledge and expertise.

Claire wondered if he had registered the irony of the situation. Dr. Jack Brady, the only man she had ever loved, the only man she would ever love, was a world-renowned kidney specialist, and their child, the product of that love, had the worst kind of kidney disease.

She answered the question at last. "He's my ex-husband."

The doctor shifted uncomfortably. "I'm sorry. I didn't mean to intrude on your personal life."

Claire didn't need to say anything in reply. The past was past, and just because she was coming here didn't mean that anything had changed between her and Jack. Their relationship was over, and would remain over. There was nothing left to salvage—if indeed there had been anything in the beginning. Yet she kept staring at her daughter and seeing Jack as he'd been when she first met him. Jack at the hospital, so concerned about her finger. Jack sewing up her cut. She still had a tiny scar near where she had worn her wedding band, and she touched it, rubbing her finger across it, remembering.

She had just turned twenty-one when they met. She'd come to Minnesota with her college roommate for a visit, and had cut her finger on a knife. That day in the emergency room, when Jack had teased her about fainting at the sight of blood, she had laughed. Then he'd asked her on a date and they had fallen in love...made love. Meghan was a part of him, a precious life they had formed together. They'd been so happy at first, so in love, in such young love, naively believing it would last forever. When had it all gone wrong?

"Mrs. Brady?"

Claire wasn't certain how long she'd sat there thinking of the man she had loved so desperately and of their child, who was gravely ill. She jumped, startled when the doctor touched her shoulder. "Yes?"

"Did you want to get your stuff together? We've pulled up near the helicopter."

Realizing she had been daydreaming about what might have been, she turned away. She didn't have time to dwell on the past. Meghan was sick, and what had happened between her and Jack was best forgotten. Their marriage was over—undeniably, irrevocably over, and it had been over for years. She was coming here for a reason, and it wasn't to shore up a relationship that had been doomed from the start. *Then why did her hands tremble at the thought of seeing him? Why did her heart race at the mention of his name?* Refusing to acknowledge those particular thoughts, Claire smiled at the doctor.

"Oh, yes. Thanks." Claire unsnapped her seat belt and grabbed the satchel she had packed, holding it in her lap. The straight, pale gray skirt and thin red blouse she had worn were wrinkled from the trip. She brushed at the creases. "Will we all be able to go on board the helicopter?"

The doctor smiled gently. "Don't worry. It's a big chopper. Everyone should fit."

Claire hadn't realized she was so easy to read. But she didn't want to be left behind. She glanced back outside. Jack was gone. A blast of frigid air announced the fact that they had stopped moving and someone was boarding.

Moments later Jack strode up the aisle carrying his physician's bag. His cheeks were ruddy from the cold, and to Claire he seemed more handsome than ever. Except for his hands, Claire had always thought he looked more like a football player than a doctor, with his broad shoulders and rugged features, his finely chiseled nose and slim hips. He had strong hands, with long, capable fingers, the nails blunt and clean. Under his coat he wore a white shirt and dress pants—his physician's attire. The shirt was open at the top to reveal a smattering of chest hairs. At his temples a few streaks of gray blended in with the dark hair.

The plane had been specially equipped for medical transfer. A few seats for personnel had been installed behind a large cubicle that was nearly an exact replica of a hospital operating room. Bright lights hung overhead. Along the walls oxygen tanks and emergency equipment had been strapped into cabinets that contained everything from dressings to intravenous tubing. There was even a heart monitor near where Meghan slept.

Jack paused just before reaching the child and flicked his gaze to Claire. Though she saw his eyes every day, in her daughter, she'd forgotten how blue they were, how dark and intense. And she hadn't thought about how she would react to them. The moment he turned to her, her heart hit the floor and her pulse hammered in her throat. God, how she'd loved him.

"Hello, Claire."

Even though she'd talked with him last night, she'd also forgotten the low, husky tone of his voice. It was still so damned sexy. Five years ago when she had first heard him speak, she had melted. Of course, that was moments before she'd fainted in his arms, passing out when he lifted the dressing from her finger to look at her wound. It had been springtime and Minnesota had been in full bloom. The state had fooled her, just as he had. Taking a deep breath, she inclined her head politely. "Jack."

"How have you been?"

"Fine," she murmured, though she wanted to shout that she was awful. She had just been through hell with their child and she was torn up inside, not wanting to see him, not wanting to be near him, not wanting to relive the pain, yet knowing he was her daughter's only hope.

Jack nodded. "Good. We'll talk later." Then he moved on with hardly a pause.

Was that all there was between them? Polite conversation? For her part, there was no denying physical reaction. Just seeing him had caused all the old emotions to come flooding back—the love, the longing.

The regret.

Jack was now bending over Meghan to scrutinize the intravenous solution dripping into her arm. As usual, he didn't seem in the least affected by their encounter.

Though that wasn't surprising. Whether or not he was on duty, he was the consummate physician: calm, in control, clinical. The surprise was that he'd even spared a glance for Claire before he looked at his patient.

The moment the thought popped into her mind, Claire felt a pang of guilt. How could she be so nasty? She was actually sounding resentful of her own child. Jack was a good doctor; he was just too dedicated. Meghan certainly needed him more than she did, though she supposed her reaction was normal, considering the bitterness she had harbored for so long, of knowing that he had chosen medicine over her.

His entire life was the hospital. Even the night Meghan was born he'd been tied up with a patient. The birth had been traumatic, and Claire had found out later that she'd almost died—without him. She'd lain in the cold, foreign atmosphere of the delivery room, in pain and bleeding, afraid and alone. The doctors had rushed around giving her blood, trying to staunch the bleeding.

Jack had come much later, after she'd been stabilized and wheeled to her room. Distraught, regretful, carrying roses, thrilled with their tiny daughter—a little winter flower—he'd been full of apologies. His excuses had been so viable. A patient had gone into crisis. He couldn't leave, not even for his own wife. By that time the hemorrhaging had stopped and Claire was better. She'd "just" had a postpartum bleed, which had been minor compared to his patient's condition. She had outwardly laughed the incident off, appeared to understand, let him hold her, listened as he murmured words of love. But after a while, when she kept needing him and he wasn't there, she'd stopped "understanding." She'd stopped laughing. She'd grown depressed and despondent. Strange, she had fallen in love with this man because of his compassion. But in the end that same compassion had driven them apart.

She watched him now as he took in Meghan's condition. This was the doctor she was seeing. Any moment now he would take out his stethoscope to listen to Meghan's heart, then feel her pulse. He was always so organized and decisive, which was something Claire had admired in him. He'd sweep quickly down the hospital corridors making split-second assessments, even about life and death.

Jack could feel Claire observing him. He knew that despite her scrutiny, she had no idea of the discipline it took for him to turn from her. Even with his child so ill, he'd wanted to talk to Claire first, to see her, to hold her, love her, to tell her about all the agonies he had suffered without her; the hurt that night when he'd come home to find her gone, the anger that still ate at him. But he was a physician with responsibilities, and this responsibility was his own flesh and blood.

He glanced at the other doctor as he indicated Meghan. "Did she travel well?"

"She did great. She's a real little trooper."

"Any problems?"

"None."

Meghan opened her eyes when Jack touched her shoulder. A smile transformed her face. "Daddy?" she said shyly. "Is that you? Hi, Daddy."

"Hey, pumpkin," he answered, scooping her up and hugging her tightly. He laid her back down gently, as though he thought she might break. "What is this? I thought you were coming to visit me in the summer."

"I got sick, Daddy," Meghan said. "Are you gonna make me well?"

Claire could tell that this was another of those moments when Jack could let down his guard and lose control. He didn't answer right away. When he did, his voice was gruff. "I don't know, Meghan. I'm sure going to try."

"I don't like being sick."

"And I don't like you being sick," he answered.

Glancing toward Claire, Meghan smiled happily. "Did you see? Mommy came with me."

Jack smiled, too, only he kept his back to Claire. Apparently, like her, the event wasn't something he had been anticipating with joy. "Yes, I see that."

"She even wanted to come," Meghan offered. "I didn't even have to ask her."

The innocence of a child.

"Oh? How about that." Jack had busied himself glancing again at the needle in Meghan's hand, taking in the bruises on her arms, looking at her eyes for any signs of complications. "Say, is it warm in California?"

His daughter wrinkled her nose at him as though she knew he was teasing her. "It's *hot* in California, Daddy."

"Well, its cold here, so we're going to have to bundle you up and get you in the helicopter right away."

"Mommy said there was snow here."

Jack laughed. "There sure is, pumpkin. In fact, there's tons of it."

"Mommy hates snow."

Another blunder of innocence. Though it was hard to detect, Jack's laughter died and his expression tightened. Claire could almost see him remembering, thinking of the other things "Mommy" had hated: the loneliness, the desolate surroundings. Him. She'd detested the snowy Minnesota winter, the dreary days without human companionship, the days he'd been gone.

Sometimes it had seemed as if the cold seeped through the walls of their tiny apartment, making her feel as bleak and forbidding as the weather. Odd, she'd left him in January, the dead of winter, and here she was coming back to him at the same time of year.

"Yes, I remember," he answered tightly. "But that doesn't mean you shouldn't like it. Snow is fun."

"Oh, I love snow," Meghan exclaimed with all the logic of a four-year-old who had never seen the stuff in her life except on television or in the movies. "I want to build a snowman. A bi-ig snowman." She gestured excitedly with her hands. "My friend Tommy built one once, but mine's gonna be bigger."

"Is that so?" Jack laughed again and patted her shoulder. "Well, we'll see. We have to get you well, first."

Joy left the child's face. She looked stricken and her voice panicked. "But, can I build a snowman? I have to build it before the snow goes away."

"Don't worry, Meghan," Jack reassured her. "There's going to be plenty of snow. We have long winters here. And I'll be glad to help you."

The child beamed. "Maybe Mommy will help, too."

At last Jack looked at Claire again, his expression just as guarded as before. "Maybe," he answered. "That's up to Mommy."

So he was going to toss the ball into her court. Claire had been right: this visit wasn't going to be easy. Then again, what had she expected? Hearts and flowers and forgiveness? "Of course, I'll help," she said quickly. She tried to make her tone light. "But we have to get off the plane first, don't we?"

Meghan giggled, not sensing the charged atmosphere. "Don't worry, Mommy. Daddy will get us off the plane."

A matter of trust.

"Yes, I will," Jack said. "In just a couple of moments."

Reaching for a blanket, he started to bundle the child up. As he worked he chatted nonsense with Meghan—about Soldier, her teddy bear, the Band-Aids on her arms, the tests she'd been through. While Claire realized fatigue was making her feel alone and vulnerable, she couldn't help feeling excluded. For all the attention they paid her, she might not have been present, and although she was ashamed to acknowledge it, she felt another twinge of resentment at the easy camaraderie between the man she had once loved and their daughter. How had he known about the teddy bear? That Meghan slept with it at night? Needed it for comfort? Soldier was something special between her and her daughter and no one else, certainly not an absentee father.

Yet Claire was forced to admit that Jack and Meghan were close. Just because he had ignored Claire didn't mean he didn't care for his child. He called Meghan all the time; they'd gone on vacations together. In fact, Jack had come to California many times, squeezing in a day here, a weekend there. Once he'd come just for an hour to take Meghan to lunch. Claire had always managed to be gone. Since she and Meghan lived with her mother, she had let Annabelle face him. Oh, she was good about making the arrangements and about talking to him on the phone. She knew her daughter needed a father. But on one point she had been firm: she never wanted to *see* Jack again. And she'd stuck to her vow—until now.

"Ready?" Jack asked when he was done. With the help of the pilot, the doctor who had accompanied them on the trip started to roll the cart from the plane. Jack walked behind them. They were almost out the door when he glanced back at Claire. His expression was carefully shuttered. "Coming?"

Claire didn't want to be near him, because in the past that had been her downfall. One touch and she was in an embrace. Yet now, she had little choice since he held out his arm as though to help her.

"Yes." Tossing a sweater around her shoulders she stepped forward, bracing herself for his touch. It was all that she had anticipated. She shivered as he placed his hand on the small of her back. Together they walked out the door and down the steps of the airplane.

"Cold?"

Didn't he realize that her reaction wasn't from the weather? His hand seemed to burn through the thin cloth of her sweater. He'd always had the ability to set her senses afire.

"A little," she answered.

"You should have brought a parka. The weather's been beastly."

"I don't have one."

"That's right. You live in California."

She glanced at him, surprised at the bitterness in his tone. "What do you mean by that?"

"Nothing. I'm sorry." There was a long, awkward silence. Finally he asked, "How's your mother?"

"Fine. And your family?"

"Great. I hear you went to Disneyland on Christmas Day. Did you have a good time?"

More polite conversation. Claire wanted to scream at him, telling him how hurt she was. How angry and afraid. How much she had missed him. How much she had loved him. How much she had resented his dedication to medicine and the long hours without him. Instead she said, "Disneyland was fun. Meghan always enjoys it. What did you do?"

"I had an emergency case. I spent the day in the operating room."

"As usual." The words slipped out before she could stop them.

He arched an eyebrow at her. "I suppose I deserved that. However, the man did live."

"I'm glad."

"You've changed, Claire. You're harder."

What did he expect? She was no longer a young, naive girl in love with a senior resident, willing to take whatever crumbs of affection he would toss at her whenever he had the time to toss them. She was a woman; a mother with a sick child. But she was behaving badly. "I'm sorry, Jack, I don't mean to be difficult. I'm just upset about Meghan."

"I understand. I'm upset, too." They had reached the helicopter. Pausing, he turned to her. "Claire?"

The rotors were so loud she could hardly hear, but the husky tone of his voice thrilled through her. She glanced up at him. Something flashed in his eyes—some deep emotion she couldn't quite read.

"Yes?"

Jack stared at her for a long moment. He wanted to grab her and shake her. No, he wanted to grab her and kiss her senseless. God, how he loved this woman, would always love her, but she held herself so aloof. Had he hurt her that badly? Sometimes he still didn't understand what had happened between them, where it had all gone wrong. By the time he'd realized how unhappy she was, it was too late. No matter how much he needed answers, this was hardly the time to approach their problems, out here on the runway with the snow and wind blowing and their child sick.

He shook his head. "Never mind. I'll help you inside." Taking her hand, he boosted her up into the seat. "Be sure and strap yourself in."

"I will."

Turning away, he jumped in the back with Meghan. As soon as he gave the word the helicopter lifted off, heading for the hospital. Wondering what he'd wanted, Claire sighed and pulled her sweater tighter, glancing out at the city below. When she had lived here the area had seemed like one vast, frozen wasteland. Apparently nothing had changed. It was as cold and forbidding today as it had been the day she'd left.

Inside the helicopter the noise was deafening. She couldn't hear what Jack and Meghan were saying, but her daughter was laughing. At least they could talk, which was more than she could say about herself and Jack. They'd never been able to communicate, which was one of the reasons her marriage had fallen apart.

If they had been able to talk, things would have been different. Maybe the weather wouldn't have depressed her so. But all they'd done during their stolen hours together was make love. At first she'd tried to understand his long absence, feeling shallow and selfish if she even thought about complaining.

Then, after Meghan was born, he spent even more time at the hospital. As the days passed it became harder for her to deal with the loneliness, the frustration, and the damned cold. There were moments when she'd felt as if the weather had possessed her, had turned her into some unthinking, unfeeling stranger, even to herself.

She had been young when she married Jack. She should have known when they'd ended up back at the hospital every time they had a date what it would be like married to him, but she'd fallen in love with him. The day she was due back at UCLA she had quit college to marry him, willing to make him her life.

But his career had always come first and she had been all alone in an atmosphere foreign to her. Like their daughter, Claire had never seen snow before she lived in Minnesota. The long, bleak winter had depressed her. Every day she'd gotten increasingly despondent. By the weather. By Jack. Then one day, stranded in the cold apartment by a raging blizzard and trying to comfort a screaming, colicky baby, she'd simply had enough. She'd decided to leave. As soon as she could make arrangements to get out of the city, she'd bundled Meghan up and gone home to her mother in California. It had taken Jack three days to come home from the hospital and notice that she was gone.

He had called, but she refused to talk to him, and he hadn't cared enough to come and get her. Jack would always be devoted to his craft, and Claire accepted that now. Not that the knowledge would have made any difference in their relationship. They'd been doomed from the start as two people too far apart in their needs. Yet sometimes the memory of his touch was so vivid that she could feel him beside her, kissing her, loving her, running his hands possessively over her body.

Suddenly, Claire caught herself and sat up straight in the seat. She couldn't keep thinking this way. If she wasn't careful she'd be back in his arms, making the same mistakes all over again, loving him and being closed out of his life. Yet she couldn't help the memories. Nor could she help loving him.

The realization that she still loved Jack didn't really come as a surprise to Claire. For a moment she was stunned and panic stricken. She wanted to grab Meghan and get back on the plane to California and safety. But in reality she'd known all along that she'd never gotten over him. She loved him with every fibre of her being. Leaving him had been easier because she told herself she didn't love him. Now, face-to-face, it was difficult to keep pretending. So how was she going to protect her emotions? This time she had no choice. No matter what happened, she couldn't go home. She had to stay here— for Meghan's sake.

With another heavy sigh she glanced back at her daughter and ex-husband. They were still laughing and talking animatedly. Finally accustomed to the rotor noise, Claire could make out their conversation. "That's silly, Daddy," Meghan was saying. "Stop fooling me."

"Nothing silly about it."

"You can't reach for a star." Meghan had been excited about seeing the stars "close up" from the airplane, and apparently she'd shared that excitement with Jack.

"Sure, you can," he answered. "If it's the right star."

"How?" Meghan was still the doubting Thomas. "How are you going to get a star?"

"Just reach right up and grab it. Whip it right out of the sky. Boom! It's yours." Fist folded, he grasped his hand into the air in demonstration and opened it to blow it at her like a kiss.

Although Meghan giggled, she wasn't convinced. "There's no star there."

"Didn't you feel it?"

"No."

Claire smiled. She realized that Jack was speaking philosophically, equating the heavens with goals, but Meghan didn't understand. Convincing her very stubborn, very logical daughter was going to be difficult. "Okay," he went on, tweaking her nose. "Let's see. It's kind of like pretend. You have to believe that it's there."

"What kind of stars are there?"

He furrowed his brow. He always did that when he was thinking. So many nights she'd lain in his arms, caressing his brow, tracing the lines around his eyes, the tiny laugh lines. "All kinds," he told her. "There are stars of hope and there are stars of love."

"Like I love you and you love me?"

He nodded. "Right."

"What else?" she probed.

"Well." He shrugged. "There are stars of special love." Suddenly he glanced at Claire. Their gazes met and held, his a dark blue, hers a pale imitation. "I had a special star once," he went on softly. "A special star of love."

"What happened to it?" Meghan asked.

Jack kept staring at Claire. Somehow she realized he wasn't talking to their child. He was talking to her, and he was talking about the end of their marriage. "I don't know," he said. He smiled ruefully. "It flew away."

"Perhaps it was driven away," Claire couldn't help but say.

His gaze didn't waver. "Perhaps," he agreed. "Or perhaps it just didn't care enough to stay."

Was that what he thought? How could he not have known she'd loved him! Thankfully, moments later the helicopter touched down on the roof of a tall building. "We're here," the pilot announced. "Beautiful downtown Minneapolis. County General Hospital."

As the man finished speaking, the back doors opened and a complete medical crew of more doctors and nurses in one spot than Claire had ever seen rushed up. With one final glance her way, Jack turned and helped escort their daughter out of the helicopter toward a waiting elevator. Claire stood by and watched as he disappeared into the building with Meghan.

No, this wasn't going to be an easy trip.

Chapter 2

Claire stood on the hospital roof for several long moments, watching them leave. Finally a nurse touched her shoulder and directed her toward the admissions office. For the next several hours she answered a deluge of questions and signed what seemed like countless forms. By the time she made her way to the fourth floor to find her daughter, she was feeling the effects of several nights without sleep and a long airplane ride, as well as dealing with the emotional turmoil of seeing Jack. No matter how difficult she had thought this trip would be, what she'd imagined didn't compare with the reality of her reaction to him. How in the world was she going to get through this mess?

Once on the kidney unit, Claire stopped at the nurses' station for directions. Everyone was busy, but several people turned as though to assess her. It was apparent they knew she had once been married to Jack. He had told her often enough that gossip spread quickly in a hospital. Apparently the grapevine had been fruitful.

"Hello, Mrs. Brady," a clerk said at last. "Dr. Brady will be back in a moment. Meghan's in room 2211. It's just down the hall and to your right."

"Thanks." Claire tried to smile but everyone was staring at her so openly, almost angrily, particularly a tall, attractive redheaded nurse. Was she Jack's current love interest?

"Do you need help to find the room?" the clerk went on.

"No, I'm fine." Claire stepped away. Of course she would encounter hostility. How could she have expected otherwise? This was Jack's unit, and he was highly respected. No matter what had happened between them, his staff would be on his side, automatically blaming her for any unhappiness.

Claire entered the room to find someone already drawing blood from Meghan's arm and a nurse bustling around the room, settling her belongings and bringing in a breakfast tray. As a kidney patient Meghan was on a high-protein, fluid-restricted diet. Since they were letting her eat, they apparently couldn't be doing any other tests today. Although the child had slept most of the night, she looked tired, pale and drawn. But she didn't complain. When Claire walked in she was telling her roommate, a girl who looked to be around fifteen years old, all about the helicopter ride.

"It's real fun. You lift straight up in the air."

"Yeah?" The teenager popped a bubble from her chewing gum—one of the few treats a kidney patient could have because of their restricted diet—obviously unimpressed. "Awesome."

"We saw the stars."

"Cool."

The nurse smiled at Claire. "Oh, Mrs. Brady, Dr. Brady said to explain that we don't have private rooms. This is a kidney unit and we have adult patients, too."

"Fine."

"We put Meghan in with Kathleen," she went on as the lab technician left. "We think they'll get along well." The nurse lowered her voice. "Kathy doesn't say much, but she's a pleasant girl. Her parents have to be away for the next few weeks and we thought she might be lonely."

The teenager in the next bed was pretty. She had long blond hair, dark brown eyes, and was just beginning to develop curves. She *didn't* say much. She was too busy popping her gum and watching television. But Claire could tell she was sick; her complexion was similar to Meghan's and she had bruises up and down her arms.

"Totally," the girl said now, answering some comment of Meghan's. She glanced at Claire. "Hey. Did the nurse call you Mrs. Brady?"

Claire nodded. "Yes."

"Are you married to Dr. Brady?"

That seemed to be the question of the decade. "I was."

The nurse arched an eyebrow. "Kathleen, I don't think that's any of—"

"Awesome," the teen cut in. She popped another bubble, enthusiastically now. "He's a hunk."

Obviously that was another popular opinion. The nurse turned to Claire. "A little hero worship," she explained in low tones. "I'm sorry. She doesn't mean to embarrass you."

"I understand," Claire whispered back. And truthfully, Jack was a hunk. She'd never denied that he was a devastatingly attractive man. All she'd complained about was his total dedication to medicine.

The teenager turned to Meghan. "He your dad?"

"Uh-huh."

"Cool. Hey, wanna watch cartoons?"

Apparently Meghan was accepted, and as with most children, cartoons were her favorite television fare. "Sure," she answered enthusiastically.

Kathleen flicked the channels. "We can catch the soaps later."

Meghan frowned. "What's soaps?"

"Soap operas. You know, love and all that junk." If nothing else, for sure her daughter was going to get an education, Claire thought as the teenager went on popping her gum and talking. "There's this totally awesome doctor on *Great Hospital*. He's nearly as handsome as Dr. Brady. Wait'll you see. Almost makes you want to be sick."

The nurse slid Meghan's breakfast tray across a table. "I'll remind you of that this afternoon when you complain about your tests, Kathleen."

"Yuk, tests. What do I have to have today?"

"X rays. No big deal."

"That's what you say!"

The nurse glanced at Claire. "Would you like a cup of coffee, Mrs. Brady? Or how about a breakfast tray? You haven't eaten, either, have you?"

"Coffee will be fine. Actually, I'm just tired. I think I've got jet lag."

"You flew all night?"

"We left Los Angeles at midnight."

"Why don't you take a nap, then? There's a lounge down the hall. Or I could let you use one of the examining rooms. They're a little more private and I could try to find one with a cot."

Claire smiled her thanks. "I'll be all right. I'd like to stay with Meghan for a while."

"I'm sure Dr. Brady will be back soon. He was called away on a consultation."

Jack was always being called away on a consultation—or to the emergency room or to Intensive Care or to another unit or to another hospital. He was always busy. Claire nodded. "Fine. I'll just wait, then, if you don't mind."

The nurse bustled away.

Meghan was almost too tired to eat. After a few bites of egg, she placed her fork down. Her eyes batted sleepily. "Did you see the snow, Mommy? It was all over the ground."

"I sure did."

"When we were on the helicopter, Daddy told me every snowflake is different."

"Yes," Claire answered. "The shapes are all different."

"I'd like to see one up close," the child said wistfully. "Will we be here long enough for me to see one?"

Claire wished she could say they would be here for a few hours, but she knew that wasn't true. Considering Meghan's diagnosis, they would probably be in Minneapolis for several months. "I'm sure we will."

"Is Daddy coming back?"

"I'm right here, Meghan," Jack said, striding into the room, his long white lab coat flying out behind him. Several other doctors followed him, trotting behind him like he was the Messiah and they were the disciples. "This is my daughter, Meghan," he said to them. "Honey, meet the doctors assigned to your case."

As unpleasant as her illness was, at least Meghan's hospitalization had gone smoothly. Despite all the tests she'd been through, she wasn't afraid of doctors. She smiled shyly at the row of physicians and turned to Jack. "Can I go to sleep now, Daddy? Or do I have to go for a test?"

"No tests today," he promised, bending over to give her a kiss. "And, yes, you can go to sleep. Mommy and I need to talk, anyhow."

"Oh-la-la," Kathleen muttered under her breath. "A consultation."

Several doctors smiled. Even Meghan grinned, though Claire doubted her daughter had understood the teenage girl's innuendo. Jack just shook his head. On his way out of the room, he winked at Kathleen and patted her knee. "Smile pretty for your X rays, Kathy."

"Sure thing, Doc."

At the door he turned and swept out his arm as he had before, on board the helicopter. "Coming?"

Claire's heart pounded in anxiety. From the look on his face, she knew the consultation was going to be about Meghan and that it was going to be serious. Reluctant to leave the child, she bent down and brushed back a lock of dark hair. "I won't be long, sweetheart."

"Mommy?" Meghan called as Claire got to the door. "See if it's started snowing out again. Okay?"

Minneapolis had just endured one storm. Claire doubted that even here, nature would be so fickle as to dump another one back-to-back. "And if it is?"

"Could you bring me a snowflake?"

She laughed. How could a California girl be so excited about snow? But Meghan was a child, and curious. "Tell you what—if it's snowing out, I'll bring you a whole bowlful."

Once in the hall, the entourage of doctors scattered in all directions. Jack led Claire to his office on the floor, just down the hall from the nurses' station. Although the room was spacious, books and framed certificates lined the walls, making it appear crowded. Aside from a desk and two chairs, the only other furniture was a sofa that sat in a darkened corner, probably for those nights he didn't make it home. A model of a human kidney decorated his desk.

"Have a seat." He closed the door behind them and gestured to one of the chairs.

"Thanks." Nervously Claire tucked her skirt beneath her. "This is nice."

"It's home." He glanced up at her. "But you probably already know that."

Claire shrugged, not remarking. No sense in being testy. For a moment, neither of them spoke. Finally Jack cleared his throat. "I've had a chance to review Meghan's chart from L.A. General," he started right in.

Claire's heart plummeted to the floor. "Is Meghan—"

He held up his hand. "Let me finish."

"I'm sorry."

"Claire, Meghan is a very sick child, but I haven't found anything yet because I haven't done anything yet. You can relax. Okay?"

"I'm just so worried."

"I know," he said sympathetically. "I'm worried, too, and I'm going to take care of her. If it's all right with you, there are a few tests I'd like to repeat."

She would be a fool to object. The man was an expert. "Of course. Anything."

"I don't want to expose her to needless radiation," he went on, "or further prodding, but I would like to see if we get any different results."

"I understand."

"I'll need you to sign some papers. They'll have them at the nurses' station."

"Fine."

Taking out his pen—the gold-plated one he always carried in his shirt pocket—he scribbled a note on the chart. "I'll tell Hal to schedule X rays for tomorrow morning. Did you meet Hal Davies?"

"No."

"I'm sorry. I'll introduce you later. Anyhow, while Dr. Davies will be the physician of record, I'll be following Meghan closely. In the meantime, you're going to need a place to stay. I wondered if you wanted to check in across the street."

She frowned. She hadn't considered where she would stay, except that it wouldn't be with him. "Is there a hotel or something across the street?"

"Not quite a hotel. More like a dormitory. A few months ago we opened Care House. It's a building we bought and converted into rooms for kidney families. Since most of our patients are chronically ill and many are from out of state, I wanted someplace for their relatives to stay. It's not very fancy, but it's close by, and you can come see Meghan at any time."

That had been one of his dreams, Claire remembered—to find some way to house families. Apparently it was a dream he'd realized.

"Doesn't the hospital have visiting hours?"

"Not on my unit. I try to make the hospital stay as easy as possible for the families as well as my patients, and that means being accessible at all times. There is a hotel a few miles north of here, if you'd be more comfortable there," he went on. "I'll be glad to call."

Claire shook her head. "No. Care House sounds great."

"Good, I'll make the arrangements." He picked up a phone and dialed, speaking quickly to someone, giving them her name. Then, hanging up, he scribbled a note on a chart. "All set."

"That's it?" Claire asked.

He glanced at her. "That's it about Meghan. You look tired, Claire."

"I am. It was a long trip. I'll get some rest later."

Jack shifted in his chair, not sure he should continue. "Feel like talking?"

She frowned at him. "About what?"

"Us."

Hearing that single word made her heart thud. Aside from Meghan's illness, their relationship was the last thing she wanted to discuss. She'd already lived the pain of the long, lonely nights without him. She didn't want to face all that again. "There's nothing to talk about, Jack."

"Sure, there is," he said. "There's lots to talk about."

She swallowed hard, knowing full well what he was getting at. "Like what?"

"Like what happened between us. Claire, why wouldn't you speak to me all these years?"

Claire bristled at his tone. She had questions of her own. Why had he chosen medicine over her? Why had he left her alone night after night with a child and no one to help? Why had he excluded her from his life? "I did speak to you."

"Only to make arrangements for me to see Meghan."

"What else did you want?"

"Reasons," he said, tossing his pen down on the desk and leaning back in his chair. "Explanations. Let's take off the gloves of pretense and give each other some answers for a change. Why did you leave me, Claire?"

She sighed. "We've been through this before, Jack."

"No, we haven't." He shook his head firmly. "We haven't been through it at all. You refused to talk to me."

Claire's frown deepened. "I don't understand, Jack. Why the sudden interest? We've been divorced for four years."

He sat forward in his chair. "I was interested then, too. I recall asking you several times what happened. You never responded."

"I left you an explanation."

"You left me a *note*, Claire," he said, his tone terse and angry. "A note scribbled on a piece of scratch paper. You told me you were going back to California because you couldn't stand the snow. That's all. Why did you walk out on me? I think I have a right to know."

Perhaps he was right, but her hurt took over. She clenched her hands more tightly. "I don't know. I thought that if I never saw you that it would be easier."

"Then what?"

"I had to forget you. It was the only way I knew how."

"And did you forget me?"

"Yes." *No.* She sighed again. "Jack, this isn't the appropriate time to discuss our marital problems. Meghan is sick."

"Which is exactly why we have to discuss them. You're going to be here for a long time, and we need to get things clear between us. Or do you want to skirt around subjects for the next several months as we did this morning?"

"I don't have anything to say."

"Not even an explanation for leaving? For divorcing me? I thought we loved each other."

But love was an elusive emotion. It brought such pain and sadness and sorrow. Shoving her hands into her skirt pockets, Claire stood and walked to the window. It was snowing out again and the sky was white with swirling flakes. How she hated winter.

"Love isn't always an answer, Jack," she said at last, staring at a tree outside his window. Its limbs reached toward the sky, so dark and ugly, all stark and bare. "Sometimes it's a burden."

"I could have explained."

But it had been too late for explanations. That year of her life had been hell on earth. He had frozen her from his life just as the winter had frozen the lakes.

She glanced away from the window to look at him. She felt like a whining child, but he had asked. "Explained what? Your dedication to medicine? You didn't have time for me, Jack. I was a burden, and so was Meghan."

"I'm sorry for hurting you, Claire. I didn't know you were feeling that way."

"Which was exactly the problem to begin with. You didn't know anything about me." And he hadn't cared enough to learn. "Jack, I came to Minnesota to get medical treatment for our daughter. That's all. I don't want to discuss our relationship." Yet she somehow felt selfish standing here and accusing him of ignoring her. The man was noble. He *helped* people.

"You're that bitter?"

She steeled herself to his gentleness. He had always been so persuasive. But she was older and wiser now, and she wasn't about to get involved. "Look, Jack, I'm quite willing to put aside our differences because we have to get along, but I don't want to discuss our past or what happened between us. It's a moot point. We couldn't solve it then, and I doubt we could solve it now."

"We couldn't solve it because you left."

She whirled around to face him, finally losing control. "What did you expect me to do?" she exclaimed. "I had a baby, for God's sake. I was alone. There wasn't any heat and I was half frozen and you weren't around!"

"You could have told me."

Obviously he wasn't going to leave the situation alone. And truly he didn't understand. If he had loved her, he would have known. "I don't want to talk about the past, Jack. What do I have to do to get that across to you?"

"Why not?"

"Because it's not going to get us anywhere."

"Because you still love me?"

Quickly she turned away from him. There was no way she could admit that. It would weaken her resolve.

But she could feel him behind her, sitting at his desk, watching her. "Do you still love me, Claire?"

"No."

"You're sure?"

At this moment she wasn't sure of anything, yet she couldn't let down her guard. She *couldn't* love him again, couldn't be caught in the same trap. "Yes, I'm sure."

"I see." There was a hard edge to his voice. "Can we get along for Meghan's sake?"

"I think that's imperative," she said.

"I agree."

In the silence that followed she wanted to throw herself into his arms, to ask him to hold her, to love her, to take her to the sofa and make mad, passionate love to her the way he had those years ago when he'd come home to her in the middle of the night, so tired from his duties. The way he had the night they'd met. Why was she so bogged down in memories?

"Claire?"

"Yes?"

"You weren't the only one hurt."

She studied him for a long moment—the blue of his eyes, the sincerity of his expression. He looked so vulnerable. Odd, it had never occurred to her that he'd been hurt by their breakup. Jack was invincible, he was strong, in control. "I'm sorry, Jack. I didn't mean to hurt you."

"People don't mean to do a lot of things. I didn't mean to leave you alone. It just happened."

"You didn't come to California to get me." The words were an accusation more than a statement.

"I had a residency to finish. I had responsibilities."

"That always meant more than me."

"God, Claire! Did you expect me to just pick up and leave?" he asked incredulously. "What did you want me to do? Toss my scalpel in a corner and catch the next plane out? I came to California as soon as I could."

"To see Meghan."

"I came to see you," he said.

For a moment all she could do was stare at him in surprise. "Please don't—"

"All those trips were to see you," he cut in angrily. "But you were never home. You always had something to do. You were working or you were shopping or you had an appointment. What was I to think?"

She walked back to the window, not knowing what to think herself. So what if he had come to see her? It had been months later. "It was too late."

"We could have discussed it."

"For what? Our marriage was over."

"According to you. I had no idea it was in trouble."

"Oh, come on, Jack," she said. "Don't give me that. You knew I was unhappy."

"I knew you were upset about the weather. I didn't think you would walk out on our marriage over it. It was just a snowstorm."

"It was a blizzard," she corrected. "A lousy, rotten blizzard. And I was stuck *alone* for three days."

"Claire, people don't walk out on their marriages over a blizzard," he said calmly. "Usually it takes something else. Something a little more critical."

"You're right," she answered, calm now, too. "It *was* something more critical. Jack, don't you see what the storm represented to me?"

"No," he answered honestly. "Frankly, no. I don't."

"Then there's no sense going into it." She shook her head. "I don't want to argue with you, Jack. This isn't doing either of us any good. What's done is done. You feel wronged. I feel wronged. Let's just let it go."

"You can forget that easily?" he asked in that husky tone of his that drove her wild. "Just throw away what we had?"

"Don't you understand, Jack? We didn't have anything. At least, not from my point of view." She folded her arms around her body in an instinct of self-preservation. "Oh, sure, we had sex," she said. "I'll give you that. But a relationship is more than two strangers making love in the middle of the night. A relationship is sharing, talking, being with one another, loving."

"Dammit, Claire, I loved you," he said.

Turning away from him, she wandered to the front of his desk and picked up the kidney model to study its intricate parts. In addition to all the other strikes against them, once they'd gotten married, they'd discovered how little they had in common. Although she wasn't squeamish anymore, what could a man who wanted to share his surgical experiences with his wife say to a woman who

fainted at the sight of blood? Claire liked the arts—
reading, painting. Medicine and science were foreign to
her. The only things Jack ever read were textbooks and
medical journals.

Then there was his family: his Italian mother and Irish
father, scads of aunts and uncles and cousins, and children who ran around. Whenever Claire went to his parents' house, the kids would be laughing and screaming
while the adults chatted more and more loudly. Everyone gestured wildly. As an only child, she'd never been
exposed to anything remotely like it. Her family get-
togethers had been quiet, sedate; consequently, when he
took Claire to visit his parents', she'd sat in a corner,
stunned, not knowing what to think, wanting to protect
her unborn child from an accidental blow from those
gesticulating arms.

As the youngest in his family, Jack had been the
bright, shining hope for the future. The professional in
the family. The *doctor*. Jack Brady, M.D., of the Bradys.
At holidays they would pass the hat for Jack, each person in his family happily tossing in grocery money or
savings to subsidize his education.

"We love you, Jack," his brother would say.

"We're counting on you," his sister would add.

A wife and child had increased his financial burden.
He'd never said anything, but he'd always been silent on
the way home from their visits. Claire had felt guilty,
particularly when his mother pointed out how difficult
things were for him. Yet if Claire mentioned finding
work, he got upset. Sometimes he was so traditional, so
macho. He wanted to support his wife and child fully, but
he was only a resident, whose salary was meager unless
he could pick up extra hours. She had tried to tell him
that money didn't matter, what she needed was him. But

Jack hadn't listened, and he remained intent on his goals—to save the world.

She set the kidney model back down. "And I loved you. But it's over. Can't you see that?"

He stared at her for the longest time, his blue eyes so dark and intense. Then he said softly, so softly she could hardly hear, "It's only over if you want it to be over."

With a sigh, Claire pushed her hair back from her face. "I don't intend to start this all over again. I'm not going to go through it. All I want is for you to help Meghan."

"I will help Meghan. I think you know that. But this doesn't have a thing to do with our child. This is between us—me and you—and this is one time I'm not going to let you deny reality."

"I'm not denying anything."

"No? Try again. I have a lot of faults, Claire. I know that. I'm too dedicated. I care too deeply. But you have some bad habits, too, one of which is to pretend something doesn't exist, particularly if that something makes you uncomfortable. You can't wish our relationship away."

"There's nothing to wish away. That's what I've been trying to tell you, Jack. We don't have a relationship."

"Yes, we do," he answered. "If it's only the fact that we share a child."

He was getting too close to her, probing too deeply. Claire knew she had to convince him to leave her alone. She had to say something to make him listen—for both their sakes. For Meghan's sake. "And that's all we share. That's all we'll ever share. I told you before, Jack, I don't love you. What do I have to do to convince you?"

Once again he seemed hurt and angry. He stared at her as though assessing the truth of her statement. "Don't—"

"I don't love you," she repeated firmly. "Please don't make me say it again."

Her plea must have gotten to him. He sighed. "Well, you can't get much clearer than that, can you?"

"I'm sorry."

"So am I," he said. A knock at the door interrupted the tense moment. Jack glanced at the wood structure as though it were a foreign object. "Yes?" he called.

The red-haired nurse Claire had noticed before opened his door and stepped inside. According to her identification badge, her name was Nancy Ferguson. "Excuse me," she said, holding out a chart. "I don't mean to disturb you, Dr. Brady, but I wondered if you'd clarify this order. I think it's for an intravenous solution, but I can't seem to make it out."

"Let me see." Jack went over to her and glanced at the page. "It's D5W. Dextrose in water."

She leaned over his arm. "Oh. The *W* looked like an *R*."

"Sorry, I was in a hurry."

"No problem," she returned with a smile. "Just so I get it right. I decided long ago that all you doctors need a handwriting course."

"How's Robbie Parker doing?" He went on without a pause. "Is he back from dialysis yet?"

"Yes. He's fine. He lost five pounds."

"And his electrolytes?"

"Within normal range."

"Great. Better keep a close eye on him tonight, though," Jack told her. "Since this is his first time being dialyzed, he might get weak."

"Right."

The nurse was very pretty, Claire thought: tall and vivacious, with freckles and bright green eyes. From the way she was looking at Jack, it was obvious they'd had a relationship at one time, perhaps still had. It was also obvious that the nurse was very much in love with him. Reading Jack was more difficult. He seemed friendly enough, but professional, holding himself slightly aloof. Yet he had always been a private person. If they were an item, Claire doubted he would want the entire hospital to know it.

"Let's get another set of electrolytes on him later on tonight," Jack was saying.

"Around eight okay?"

"Fine."

He had turned away when the nurse placed a hand on his arm. "Jack, I wanted to tell you . . . I met Meghan a few minutes ago. She seems like a sweet girl. I'm sorry she's so sick."

He nodded. "Thanks."

The nurse glanced at Claire and smiled, obviously looking for an introduction. Either Jack was incredibly naive or else he was dense, for he didn't seem to notice at all. "By the way," he asked, "did you happen to get any results back yet from Meghan's blood tests?"

The nurse shook her head. "No. Nothing yet."

"Be sure and page me as soon as you do."

"Right." The nurse turned to Claire again, this time dropping all pretense of subtlety. She held out her hand. "Mrs. Brady? I'm Nancy Ferguson."

"I'm sorry," Jack said, as if he had truly forgotten. "This is my ex-wife, Claire." Then he smiled at the nurse and placed his hand on her shoulder. "Nancy is one of our best nurses. She'll take good care of Meghan."

Claire inclined her head politely. "It's nice to meet you."

"It isn't really, considering the circumstances," the nurse answered, but her expression was so cheerful that Claire couldn't tell if she was being facetious or genuinely caring. "I'm sorry Meghan's sick. I'll watch her closely."

"Thank you."

Lowering her voice, the nurse glanced at Jack with a hopeful expression. "See you later?"

Jack nodded. "Right."

Now more than ever, Claire was certain they were lovers. Strangely she felt pangs of regret and loss. How could he have betrayed her with another woman? Yet that was silly. She didn't have any claims on Jack. It wasn't any of her business if he had made love with this woman or with hundreds of women.

Still, she couldn't prevent her feelings. She wanted to ask if they were in love—or rather, if he was in love—but the phone rang and she didn't get to ask him anything for several more minutes. When he hung up he turned to her. "I'm sorry, I'd like to talk longer, but I have to go."

She nodded. "I understand."

"No, you don't," he countered, but he held open the door for her. "Come on, I'll take you to Care House. If we use the walkway you won't have to worry about a coat."

"I can get there by myself," Claire said.

Jack shook his head. "I'll take you."

The decision was made for them when a woman from the admissions office caught up with them. "Oh, Mrs. Brady," she called. "I've been trying to find you. I have some more papers for you to sign. Could you come back down to admitting?"

"I was going to take her across the street," Jack said.

"Why, I can take her, Dr. Brady," the woman volunteered. "You're such a busy man. You shouldn't have to do those things. And I can give her a tour of the hospital, too, after she signs the papers."

It all sounded logical and while she didn't welcome signing any more papers, Claire was happy to get a respite from Jack. Going to Care House with him would involve another conversation, and at the moment she wasn't up to sparring with him. Then again, he was the doctor. She glanced at him.

"You'd better go," he said. "I have some things to do, anyhow. By the way, if you get a chance, drop by the lab so they can draw your blood. We need to have your blood type on record just in case."

Just in case Meghan has to have surgery. But he didn't say that.

"Jack—" Claire paused. At least she owed him her allegiance. Considering everything that had transpired, she hadn't had a chance to tell him how much she appreciated all that he was doing. "Jack, I'm glad Meghan's in good hands."

He smiled that rueful grin he'd used in the helicopter, so full of regrets. "So am I, Claire. Very glad." He paused. "Although Meghan isn't the only person I'm worried about." And then he walked away.

Chapter 3

Claire didn't see Jack again until later that night. She'd gone to the admitting office and then down to the laboratory to have her blood drawn. Next she'd checked in at Care House, but she had come back to the hospital to be with Meghan. Claire had brought a bowl of snow. Kathleen was in rare form, laughing and joking, and they'd had a mini-snowball fight—if two children throwing melting flakes at one adult was considered a fight. After that they'd played quiet games, spelling and flash cards, and then all three had slept. The nurse mentioned a unit meeting but, unable to stay awake, Claire had nodded off in the chair at her daughter's bedside, the same way she had at the hospital in Los Angeles. Later they watched television.

Around eight Jack came into the room, alone this time but wearing his long white lab coat. Apparently he was still on duty. If it weren't for the creases around his eyes, which were etched just a tad deeper than they were this morning, Claire would have sworn he was just starting the day. He'd always had so much energy—and he'd always looked so sexy. Right now his olive complexion contrasted with the white coat. His hair was mussed as though he'd raked his hand through it to keep it back off his forehead. Had he slept on the sofa in his office? Taken a quick nap the way he had so many times when they'd been together? Back then, she would crawl into bed with him, kiss him, let him make love to her.

She turned away, trying to forget. Both Meghan and Kathleen were asleep. Claire had turned off the television and was getting ready to go to Care House. The hospital room was quiet and she didn't know what to say to him or how to act. Their conversation had ended on such a tense note this afternoon. Would he be angry at her—still resentful, not understanding their breakup?

But Jack acted as if nothing had happened. He glanced at both children and smiled. Then he turned to Claire, doctor to parent. "Would you like to go to the unit meeting? Or are you too tired?"

She was exhausted, but earlier the nurse had explained that two or three times a week Jack interacted with the patients and their families in order to interpret laboratory values, to answer questions or to just offer support. Tired or not, she wanted to learn everything she could about her daughter's illness, and she wanted to go.

"I thought I'd missed it. Meghan's asleep. Does that matter?"

Jack shook his head. "Most of my younger patients sleep through the meeting. You can go without her. It's really for the parents, anyhow. It would be nice if you met everyone. We kind of offer each other mutual support here, and getting to know the others is usually a good idea."

"I'd like that," Claire answered as he reached for a chart at the end of Meghan's bed. Up close she could tell that he was as tired as she was feeling. A dark stubble of beard shaded his face, and his deep blue eyes were cloudy with fatigue. Of course he'd been up for hours, and he'd probably worried about their daughter most of last night. "Did you get any results back yet for Meghan?"

He set the chart back in its rack. "Only her blood work. Everything was within the limits that I anticipated. Don't worry, Claire," he said, turning and holding out his arm, waiting for her to follow. "As soon as I get everything back, we'll talk."

That was what worried her, but she nodded, grabbed her purse and fell into step behind him. "Where are we going?"

"Down the hall to the solarium." As they left the room, he placed his hand on the small of her back, as he had so many times that day. Unfortunately she wasn't prepared this time for his touch, and she jumped as though she had been burned.

He glanced at her. "Something wrong?"

"No." She kept walking, trying to ignore the currents that curled up her spine, the heat from his body.

"Cold again? Don't you have a sweater?"

"I left it across the street."

"This won't take long. You'll be able to go to Care House soon."

"I'm fine, Jack." *Just affected by you, by your touch. Needing and wanting you.*

They walked a few more steps. "My mother wants to come to visit Meghan," he said suddenly. "I thought I'd better check with you first."

The way he had phrased the question, Claire realized he remembered she hadn't gotten along with his parents. "She knows Meghan and I are here?"

"Yes. I called her last night after I talked to you."

"What does she want?"

"Just to see her granddaughter."

Claire felt guilty about her thoughts. His mother was an old woman. Just because they hadn't gotten along didn't mean that she should punish Meghan's grandmother. "That would be fine. I'm sure Meghan will enjoy seeing her."

"Thanks, I'll tell her."

"Tell her to come anytime."

He nodded again. "I will. I know she'll appreciate it." He glanced at her, assessing her a moment. "Did I happen to mention this morning that my brother Mark and his wife Lucy finally had a baby boy?"

"Really?" Claire smiled at him, forgetting for a moment that they had argued only hours ago. "That must have made your father happy." There had been fifteen grandchildren in his family, all girls. And Lucy already had a pack of kids.

"He was thrilled. Someone to carry on the name."

"Is the baby going to be a doctor?"

Jack laughed. "If my mother has anything to say about it. She's already started the college fund. Every time I go there she says, 'Chip in for Markie.'"

Claire laughed with him. All of a sudden she wondered if he regretted all the hard work, the sacrifices he had made to achieve his goals; the sacrifices his family had made for him. It had to have been difficult for him, trying to live up to their expectations. But he had done it, and more. He had made a success of himself.

If only their personal life hadn't failed.

"Jack, I'm sorry things didn't work out between us," she blurted out. "And I'm also sorry your family was hurt."

Oddly, he smiled. "They weren't hurt, exactly. They just couldn't understand it. No one had ever found fault with me before."

Although he acted lighthearted, Claire didn't find his remark funny. "Do they hate me?"

"No one could hate you, Claire," he said. "I don't even hate you. I just wondered what went wrong."

"Maybe we were too young," she answered. When she'd come here she'd had a whole list of reasons for their breakup. Now she couldn't think of a single one that sounded convincing.

"Maybe."

Neither said anything else as they kept walking down the hall, her heels making sharp clicks on the tile floor, his crepe soles squeaking slightly. Despite the absence of the younger patients, the solarium was crowded. Everyone was talking animatedly when they walked into the room; parents, patients, doctors, nurses, were all sitting around on couches or in chairs. A few people perched on chair arms here and there, and on windowsills. A couple of older patients were joking with Nancy Ferguson about their surgeries, comparing scars.

"Dr. Brady," someone called. "Good evening."

They all stopped talking and smiled at Jack.

"What's up?" he asked, settling next to the red-haired nurse on the window ledge that ran the length of the room and taking a clipboard from her hands. "How is everyone?" Claire had taken a seat near the entrance. He gestured toward her. "This is my ex-wife, Claire. Most of you know my daughter Meghan is a patient. Be sure and say hello later."

Surprised by his openness, Claire glanced at him. Almost in unison everyone murmured welcomes. She sat and nodded, trying to smile through her pain, and hoping she wouldn't be the center of attention.

"Who wants to go first?" Jack asked when the sympathetic voices died down. "Anyone have any questions? Complaints? Recommendations?"

As a teenage boy raised his hand and discussion ensued, Claire realized that these people couldn't have cared less about her relationship with Jack. They were close to each other—like family—and they were worried about their conditions. And to a person, they worshiped their doctor. She found herself watching as he talked to them, using his hands, demonstrating, commiserating, patting someone on the shoulder, giving advice, support, tossing off orders to Nancy, who carefully transcribed them. It was a time of laughing and blowing off steam, a time of learning. Laboratory values were bantered about like tennis balls.

"Confusing, isn't it?" a tall, graying woman with a deep western drawl whispered from beside Claire. She was a parent, Claire was certain.

She nodded. "Very."

"You'll learn. It takes time. Just watch and listen."

"Thanks. I am." Claire smiled.

"By the way, I'm Sybil Parker," the woman went on in a whisper to introduce herself. "Robbie Parker's mother. And in case you're wondering, I'm from Montana. Are you staying across the street?"

Claire nodded. "Yes, I checked in earlier. I heard Jack mention Robbie this afternoon."

"He had dialysis today. First time. He did well." Sybil paused, glancing toward where Jack sat with Nancy Ferguson. "You know she's in love with him."

Surprised again at Sybil's bluntness, Claire gasped as she glanced at the woman sitting next to her.

"Did I shock you?" Sybil asked. "Sometimes I'm too outspoken. The accent may be Montana but the mouth is pure Parker. I figure there's no sense in hedging," she went on in explanation. "Life's too short. That's something you learn really quick, being here."

"I see." Although that was probably true, Claire wasn't certain she was ready to be so frank herself. In fact, she could hardly believe she was sitting here calmly while her private life was up for discussion.

"We're waiting for a kidney," Sybil went on. "It's hell."

Undeniably. To Claire, any time a child was sick was hell. "No donor?"

"Robbie inherited everything from me except my blood type. And my husband's dead. So we wait. Seems to be the key words around here: wait and hope."

"I'm so sorry."

"Thanks. Well?" she went on.

Claire was confused. "Well, what?"

"She's in love with him."

So they were back to Nancy Ferguson. Claire nodded as she glanced at Jack and his nurse. "Yes, I know."

"He doesn't love her, though."

Curiosity got the better of Claire. She frowned, turning back to Sybil. "How can you tell?"

"So you're worried. Good." Sybil smiled. "Nothing like a good old-fashioned love triangle. We really like Dr. Brady here, and we want him to be happy."

Claire wrinkled her forehead in puzzlement. "How can a love triangle make him happy?"

"It'll take his mind off his work."

This time it was Claire's turn to smile ruefully. "Don't count on it."

"Ah-huh, I hit upon the problem, huh?"

"Unfortunately," Claire admitted.

Sybil paused, watching Jack speak to someone for a moment. Then she turned back to Claire. "You know, this may sound trite, but I believe things happen for a reason. Maybe from a new perspective you'll learn to appreciate him."

If that were true, what an awful sacrifice, Claire thought. She had to admit that Jack was special. She had turned to watch him as he laughed at a remark from one of his patients. She hadn't seen that side of him in so long. He was brilliant, but his brilliance wasn't what impressed these people. It was his caring.

Sybil patted her hand. "Good luck. With Meghan, too. We're pulling for you."

"Thanks."

"We'll talk later," the woman said. "We better pay attention now or we're going to get in trouble. Sometimes he gives tests."

Claire laughed. "Really?"

"No. But it's not polite to whisper."

Sobering, realizing that that was true, Claire brought her attention back to Jack as he explained the functioning of a kidney.

When he was finished he asked, "Any more questions? No? Then let's have a good day tomorrow. We'll talk again Thursday."

As everyone filed out of the room, he turned to his nurse for a moment, speaking briefly to her and handing her an additional list of orders. Totally exhausted now, Claire wandered down the hall with the others. Everyone was headed for the same place, to check on their children.

Although the hospital room was darkened, moonlight streamed in through the windows, illuminating the two pale figures lying in bed, Kathleen and Meghan. Her daughter's dark hair spilled out on the pillow. For a moment Claire watched the child breathe, so easily, in and out. It was still hard to believe that her "baby" was actually sick and that she wouldn't get up and be fine, run around the room playing. Yet Claire knew that was impossible unless Jack could work some kind of miracle.

She was counting on him for a lot, she realized as he came into the room behind her. His crepe-soled shoes swished on the floor and he stopped just before the bed. "Is she all right?"

"Fine," Claire answered. "She's still asleep."

"Good. She needs rest. Are you going to Care House now?"

"Yes." She yawned. "I'm really tired. I think all these days without sleep have finally caught up with me."

"Come on. I'll walk you."

Her heart hit the floor. "Jack, is something—"

"Claire, you can't keep doing this," he cut in, apparently guessing her train of thought. "Every time I come into the room or offer to escort you somewhere, you can't think something is wrong with Meghan."

She nodded, sighing. "I know. I'm sorry. I keep overreacting."

"A common problem with 'mothers." He smiled gently. "I just figured I'd walk you over since I have to pick up a video movie from the recreation room. Did you have dinner?"

"Yes, I caught a bite in the snack bar."

"A sandwich, I suppose."

"Turkey."

"You should take better care of yourself, Claire. Eating meals is important."

"I was in a hurry."

He nodded. "I realize that, but it's not going to do Meghan any good if you get sick."

"Okay."

"Properly chastised?"

"Yes." But she smiled. At least he was giving her space. Considering their argument in his office, she had thought he might continue to push her for answers, but he hadn't. In fact, all evening he had treated her like every other parent.

For some reason she felt hurt by that realization. She didn't want to be treated like every other patient. She was his —his ex-wife—and Meghan was his child. They'd been in love *once*. Surely that made a difference.

"What did you think of the unit meeting?" Jack asked as they headed toward the overpass that connected the hospital to the other building. Years ago someone had designed a whole series of windowed passages that connected one building to another in the city of Minneapolis. It was possible to visit nearly every store in the downtown area without once stepping foot outdoors. Considering the harsh winters, that was about the smartest thing city planners had ever done. Jack had carried the theme through in connecting the hospital to the dorm.

"I found it interesting," she answered.

"I noticed you were talking with Sybil Parker."

She blushed, remembering their conversation. "Did we disrupt the meeting?"

"I was finished speaking."

"Oh, Jack, I'm sorry. We did disrupt the meeting."
She turned an even brighter shade of red. Had everyone
heard?

He laughed again. "I was just teasing, Claire. You
didn't bother me at all. I'm glad you've found someone
to talk to. Sybil is nice. And Robbie is one of my favorite
patients." They were in the middle of the overpass, and
he gestured toward the other side. "Did the admitting
clerk happen to give you the history of Care House?"

Claire nodded. "She said you finagled the building
from an old man."

He smiled. "Not quite. It was a donation."

"After you saved his wife."

His shrug was modest. "I gave her a kidney and a new
life, and she forced her husband to give me my dream."

"The building used to be an old department store,
didn't it?" Claire asked, glancing through the windows
at the outside of the structure. "I thought I recognized
it."

"Yes. It needed extensive renovations and I talked
them into donating it instead of selling." Pausing, he
gestured toward a building down the street. "Recognize
the drugstore?"

"Miller's," Claire said, smiling at the bright neon sign
flashing on and off. Strange she hadn't noticed it early
this afternoon. But then the sun had been shining and the
neon hadn't been so apparent. They had lived just
around the corner, in a one-room flat with rattly pipes
and space heating. The darned sign had nearly driven
them crazy, flashing on and off continuously over their
bed. "Is the Chinese laundry still next door?"

"Yes, Mr. Chin is still washing shirts."

"Remember your underwear?" She laughed, thinking about the time when they'd been just married. She

didn't have a washing machine and Jack had told her to send their clothes out. She'd sent them all to Mr. Chin, who had starched the whole lot until everything stood up by itself, including his jockey shorts.

Jack laughed too. "How could I forget? I had the stiffest clothes of any resident on staff. I could hardly walk." He gestured in the distance to another building. "The little restaurant's there, too. Emilio's. They still serve the best spaghetti in town."

"With garlic bread?"

"A whole loaf."

What about their apartment? Claire was afraid to ask, yet her gaze automatically found the spot where it would be. Darkness. For a moment neither of them spoke. In the window she could see their images waver: a man and a woman standing apart. Then he said quietly, "It's still there. I went by the other day and there were curtains in the window." When she still didn't speak he came up behind her. She could feel his breath on her cheek, warm and moist. "We had some good times, too, Claire. Remember?"

"Jack, don't." She swung around. She couldn't let him trap her with memories. She wanted to melt into his arms, to lean back and let him hold her, love her and kiss her, but she had to resist. Jack had hurt her.

Only now she was face-to-face with him, standing close to his body. She could feel the warmth, the heat. All she had to do was reach out and touch his chest where the dark hairs spilled from his shirt. All she had to do was reach up to touch his face. She wanted to caress his cheeks, feel the dark stubble scratch her palm; she wanted to soothe the tiredness from his eyes. Even from up here the neon sign reflected on his features. He was so tall and strong. So capable.

"Claire?" he said huskily.

She knew he was going to kiss her, and she didn't have much resistance. "It's not right, Jack," she said weakly in protest.

"We could start over."

"It wouldn't work."

"How do you know until you try?"

"It's too late, Jack. I don't want to be hurt again."

She started to step away, but he twisted her back, grasping her around her wrist and pulling her back. "Dammit, Claire."

"Jack, no. Don't."

With an uncharacteristic roughness, he slammed her up against his body. "Can't you feel it?" he murmured. "Don't tell me you can't." She could feel the hard wall of his chest, the even harder object pressing against her thighs. "It's there between us whether you want it to be or not," he went on. "It's been there all along Oh, hell," he muttered. "I'm tired of fighting."

Suddenly he pressed his lips to hers. Hard. Demandingly. Claire started to struggle but her efforts were futile. Jack was stronger and he bent her to his will, his mouth moving over hers hotly, his hands doing things to her body that shouldn't be done in public: rubbing, caressing, cupping her breasts. With a low, deep groan he dipped his tongue into the heat of her mouth, slipping it along her teeth, entwining it around hers.

Claire couldn't have prevented her response to him even if her life depended on it. She moaned and opened her mouth to him like a flower opening its petals to the sun, seeking, wanting, needing.

She wasn't certain why, but he abruptly broke the embrace. She gasped and stumbled back, feeling stunned.

He raked a hand through his hair. "God, Claire, I'm sorry," he said. "I didn't mean to do that."

Her chest was heaving so much she could hardly speak. Her lips felt bruised, punished, where he had ravaged them. He sure put a lot of effort into something he didn't mean to do, she thought. Distraught by her emotions, trying to pretend the episode had never happened, she ducked under his arm and started back across the passageway, hoping to defuse the moment. Almost gaily she glanced outside again. It was still snowing, lightly now. "Don't be silly, Jack. It was just a kiss."

"That was more than a kiss, Claire."

"Not to me," she said. "You know," she went on, gesturing toward the outside. "I should make it a point to visit Mr. Chin while I'm here. See if he remembers me."

Jack frowned at her, but he let the moment pass and followed her down the passageway. Sometimes she confused him so much that he didn't know how to handle her. She was lying about the kiss; he'd felt her response. Maybe he should confront her, push her; but he had a feeling she'd run.

"I should stop at the bakery, too," she said. "I've missed the rolls."

Sighing, Jack caught up with her. The only choice was to go along with her. "If you plan to go out much, you'll need to get a jacket."

She nodded. "I thought I'd go shopping tomorrow. Any recommendations?"

"Something warm. You might try red."

"*I meant* a store," she said. She tilted her head and looked at him. They'd had so many personal discussions today, what was one more. "Do you still like red, Jack?"

"I like it on you."

Once he'd given her a racy red negligee. They hadn't enough money for bus fare, but he'd splurged on the skimpy garment, just to see her in it. She still had it tucked away in a chest along with the other things he'd given her. When they reached the dorm, Jack held the door open for her, allowing her to pass. She turned sideways and scooted by. The recreation room was straight ahead; she could hear a television playing.

"What was the movie you were going to pick up?" she asked.

"Frankenstein Meets Wolfman."

"Ugh. You still like horror movies?"

He smiled. "I guess it's the little boy in me. I like to be scared."

Funny how life-and-death drama didn't frighten him. Then again, nothing really frightened him, not even the horror films. Sometimes she suspected that he watched them so he didn't have to think.

"Do you still like suspense?" he asked.

She nodded. "Yes. I guess I like to be frightened, too, only in a different way. But I've gotten more into family fare with Meghan. Shaggy dogs and fairy tales and cars that think on their own."

"I've missed that," Jack said.

Claire glanced at him, touched by his seriousness. She'd unintentionally denied him that by leaving him. "I'm sorry, Jack."

He shrugged. "It's not your fault, Claire. You don't have to bear the burden of the blame. I could have gone anyhow."

"All alone? No one goes to those movies without children."

"That bad?"

"Worse."

"Claire," he said all of a sudden. "You realize we're talking?"

She hadn't. She glanced at him. "Unusual, isn't it?"

He nodded. "But it's nice. You're a very pleasant conversationalist."

She laughed, struck by the absurdity. The perfect criterion for a relationship. *Oh, yes, I like you very much. You're a very pleasant conversationalist.* But with her and Jack it was an important milestone.

"I never could keep my hands off you," he went on.

"You didn't now," she pointed out. They stood just inside the door, each reluctant to go, but not knowing it. Claire had tucked her hands in her pockets.

"I told you I didn't mean to act like a caveman."

"You certainly did a good job."

"No, I didn't," he countered. "Or I would have dragged you by your hair kicking and screaming to your room."

"That's not your style, Jack."

"Perhaps that's where I've gone wrong," he said. "Maybe I should have been more forceful with you."

She shook her head. "Force isn't the answer."

"No? I wonder. It's odd, though. Where you're concerned, I seem to be always too little too late—or too much too soon."

Claire knew what he was saying: they'd loved each other too deeply, which made the hurt worse. Somewhere she heard a phone ring. A clerk called to him. "Dr. Brady, Miss Ferguson is on the line. She wants to speak to you."

Jack glanced over his shoulder. "I'll be right there," he said. He looked back at Claire. "I'd better be going."

"Are you going to see her?" Claire asked, all of a sudden needing to know.

"Why?"

She blushed. What had she expected? No matter how she cared, he wasn't just going to blurt out his plans for the evening. "I just wondered."

"Does it matter?"

"Why, no," she said quickly, hoping he didn't realize she was lying. "Why should it matter?"

"I don't know. You tell me."

"I was just curious," she said.

He nodded, but he must have read her mind. Or else he knew her better than she realized. "You know, Claire," he said softly, "you can lie to me forever, and you can pretend all you want, but you should at least be honest with yourself." He ran his finger gently over her bottom lip. "Good night. See you in the morning."

Chapter 4

The dormitory room that Claire had been assigned was small but comfortable. Everything was compact, including the dresser in one corner and a sink in another. Windows stretched across the front, end of the room, covered by attractive, room-darkening drapes. Aside from a bed, a nightstand and a desk, an overstuffed easy chair and a reading lamp completed the decor. The bathrooms were located down the hall.

The bed pulled at her. Had Claire not been so tired, she would probably have tossed and turned all night, wondering what would happen between her and Jack. He didn't seem content to leave their relationship alone, and that complicated matters. As it was, she hardly had the energy to take off her clothes and put on her nightgown, let alone think. Promising to unpack her things and settle in tomorrow morning, she set the alarm she found on the bedside table, fell into bed and went immediately to sleep.

The next thing she knew, the alarm was blaring and someone was pounding on her door. "Claire?" a low-pitched female voice called. "Claire, are you all right?"

The western accent was unmistakable. Claire opened her eyes groggily. God, she was tired. It seemed as if she had just closed her eyes. Yet sunlight seeped in from beneath the draperies.

Sweeping her hair back from her face, she staggered out of bed and turned off the buzzing. When she pulled open the door, Sybil Parker stood in the entrance.

The tall, attractive woman smiled. "Good morning. Are you trying to wake the dead, or just everyone who lives here?"

Claire yawned and glanced back at the alarm. "I'm sorry. I didn't hear the clock."

"Since it's been going off for the past two hours, I figured that. Want to go for breakfast?"

Two hours and no one had wakened her? Claire frowned. "What time is it?"

"Ten."

"Ten!" She glanced at her watch. "Oh, no! I wanted to get back and be with Meghan for her X rays." Shoving her hair back again, she hurried across the room toward her suitcase. "Come on in. I'd better get ready."

"There's no need to rush," Sybil told her, stepping into the room and closing the door. "Meghan's already finished with her tests. She's back in the unit."

"But I wanted to be with her," Claire said.

Sybil nodded. "I know. Dr. Brady schedules his patients for early in the morning. He figured you were sleeping and he went with her today."

Claire paused. Then Sybil was right. There was no hurry, except to see her child. "I see."

"He asked me to come check on you," the woman went on in her Montana drawl. "And to make sure you ate breakfast."

"Really?" That was awfully presumptuous of him. "Are you sure Meghan's okay?"

"She's great. Right now she's playing a game with Kathleen. Want me to wait outside while you dress?" Sybil asked. "There's not a great deal of privacy here, and I don't mean to tromp all over what little you do have."

"No, that's fine," Claire answered. "You can stay. She wasn't half as embarrassed at dressing in front of another woman as having that person know the intimate details of her personal life. So far since she'd been here, she had very few secrets because Jack had been totally open with everyone.

She pulled a pair of gray slacks and a pale pink silk blouse from the suitcase and flipped out the wrinkles. "Did Jack say anything about the X rays?"

"Just that Meghan did fine. He was due in surgery or he would have come himself to get you. He had to put a shunt in one of the dialysis patients." Noticing the mess, Sybil went to the suitcase and started hanging clothes in the closet as she talked. "Did you skip dinner last night? That kind of thing usually sets him off."

"I had a sandwich."

"Uh-oh. Cardinal sin. Fifty lashes and a walk along the gangplank."

Claire smiled. "Does everyone get his lectures?"

"Everyone," Sybil said, rolling her eyes as if she'd heard it more often than she cared to acknowledge. "The secret is to have a plateful of food whenever you see him, whether you want to eat it or not, and no circles under your eyes. Or else you get sent off to bed."

Claire laughed. "I'm beginning to think my circles are permanent."

"Well, Dr. Jack Brady will watch very closely and determine that for himself." Suddenly Sybil glanced at Claire with a stricken expression. "I'm sorry, I'm running off at the mouth here about your ex-husband, and you may not want to hear about him."

"That's all right," Claire answered. "He's not just my ex-husband anymore, he's a consultant on my daughter's case. I like knowing what's going to happen." After buttoning her blouse, she tucked it into her slacks and buckled the belt. Then she picked up a brush to run through her hair. "You mentioned yesterday that you were waiting for a kidney for Robbie. How long has it been?"

"A few weeks. We could wait months, though, there are so many people on the list. Or forever, for that matter, if a donor isn't found and Robbie gets worse." She continued to speak almost philosophically. "Did you know that over fifteen thousand people in the United States needed organ transplants last year just to save their lives?"

Claire paused, the brush in midair. "That many?"

"Yes, and fewer than one in ten got them. The really tough part is that most of those people are waiting for kidneys. Our case is further complicated by the fact that Robbie has a rare blood type, which he inherited from his father. If my husband were alive he could donate, but Ira died last year. Sometimes I just can't believe it—so much misery in one family."

"What happened?"

"Accident. He was busting a bronc and the horse threw him. Broke Ira's neck." She snapped her fingers. "It was over just like that. I guess it's better than being paralyzed, though. That would have killed him. I just wish I could have been with him. I was in the house."

How awful, Claire thought. To lose your husband and then have your child sick, too. "You mentioned you can't donate. Is it only because you're the wrong blood type?"

"Yes."

"Is that a problem?"

"In that the wait is so long."

Claire frowned. "I don't understand. Why is that bad?"

"Because each day we wait, Robbie's condition gets worse and worse. Toxins build up and he has to have dialysis, which is good these days, but unfortunately not life sustaining. If I could give one of my kidneys, Robbie could have the operation right away, while he's healthy, and a chance at a normal life—or at least a few good years."

Claire was surprised. Although she had been married to Jack, she knew very little with regard to kidney disease and transplants. She'd never found it interesting—until now. "Only a few years? Isn't a transplant like a cure?"

The other woman seemed equally surprised by her question. "No, a transplant is not a cure. Far from it, in fact. But the survival rate is good. For kidney patients the five-year rate has risen to over sixty percent."

"Just five years?" Claire was astounded. "That's all a transplant lasts?"

"Hey, it's better than it sounds," Sybil said with a smile. "There have been some patients who have gone longer—years and years, and no sign of trouble. But then there are others who have had to apply for a second transplant after a few months. Sometimes a kidney will fail on the spot; something goes wrong or it's rejected.

But with a transplant, at least the patient's got a chance. Without one, you're talking dialysis forever, and dialysis just doesn't do the job as efficiently as a kidney."

"What about the risks you mentioned with outside organs?"

"There's more of a chance of rejection."

"So an organ is better if it's donated from a family member," Claire paraphrased.

Sybil nodded. "Yes. The closer the relative, the better. Since the tissue match is generally closer, the body doesn't make antibodies to fight the organ. There's so much that can go wrong in a transplant, it's like one less strike against you. And you can operate right away, which is a real advantage."

"Will Robbie have to stay in the hospital until he gets a kidney?"

"No. As soon as he's stabilized we can find an apartment close by. He'll have to come back and forth two or three times a week to be dialyzed. At least he isn't an infant," she went on. "Those organs are the scarcest—they're more priceless than gold." She glanced again at Claire. "I'm sorry, I seem to be saying all the wrong things today. I'm sure if Meghan needs a kidney, she'll do just fine. She's what—Four? Five?"

"Four." Claire was hoping her daughter wouldn't need a kidney. She was also hoping there was nothing seriously wrong. But that was hiding her head in the sand. "How old is Robbie?"

Sybil sighed. "Fifteen. He got sick on his birthday. Ironic, isn't it? Some birthday. Hell, maybe it's a good thing I can't donate. I doubt I could pass the psychological tests. I was so mad thinking about it the other day that I put the square peg in the round hole."

"You go for counseling?"

Sybil looked surprised again. "Haven't you seen the psychiatrist yet?"

"No. Will I have to?"

"Probably. Usually everyone does, particularly if you're going to be a donor. Are you going to be a donor?"

"I don't know." Claire was discovering there was a lot she didn't know. But at least in Meghan's case, there were two parents: herself and Jack. If her daughter did have to have a kidney, she stood a better chance than Robbie.

"I go because it's kind of ghoulish sitting here and waiting for someone to die so your kid can have a chance at life," Sybil went on explaining. "The doctor helps me deal with the circumstances when I find myself torn between hope and guilt."

Claire hadn't thought about that aspect. Of course there would be guilt. "It's not like you're going out head-hunting, hoping someone will die."

"No, but there are times I feel really rotten about it. I see an automobile accident and I get excited. Or a story in the paper. Someone brain-dead, and I think, 'Hey, here's Robbie's chance.' I'll tell you, Claire, it's hell. I love that kid so much I'd give anything—I'd give my life if I could," she said in a low, intense tone, "just to make him better. But I can't. I can't do a damned thing for him."

Although Claire felt the same way about Meghan, she was surprised at the pain, the raw vulnerability, in the other woman's face. She'd seemed so tough last night, putting on a brave front; yet her feelings didn't seem odd, nor did the depth of their conversation. She hardly knew Sybil Parker, but in that moment Claire felt a closeness that even years of friendship couldn't duplicate. The two women shared one thing, and that was a bond of motherhood. They loved their children deeply. She took Sybil's hand and squeezed it in a gesture of reassurance. "I know," she murmured, "and I'm so sorry."

"Hey." Sybil laughed in a high-pitched, brittle sound, as though she were about to cry. "It's not your fault. That's the way it is—life."

"Rough."

The other woman nodded. "You can say that again. But we'll make it," she said determinedly. Her voice choked as she held back tears. "And so will our kids. Just be tough, Claire."

"I will."

Sybil shook her head almost angrily. "No, you have to be strong," she said. "You can't let anything or anyone get to you. You have to believe that Meghan's going to be fine."

"I do."

"Good." Sybil smiled, but her eyes shone brightly and she turned away. She hung the last dress in the closet and spun back around, completely in control again. "Ready for breakfast? We'd better get going or they'll have tossed out the oatmeal."

Claire smiled too. "I find it difficult to get upset over that prospect."

"Just wait," the other woman warned. "You'll regret those words."

Claire did regret her words, only she thought the eggs should have been tossed out instead of the cereal. By the time they got to the cafeteria the only food that was left were a couple of rubbery-looking yellow blotches floating in water that were supposed to be poached eggs, and a few slices of French toast. Sybil had more experience than Claire. She chose the French toast, adding mounds and mounds of butter and syrup to "kill the taste."

Claire didn't notice Jack until they sat down. He was sitting at a table near the back of the room with several other doctors. Apparently he'd just come from surgery. He wore green scrubs and a surgical cap that covered his thick, dark hair. Perhaps it was the cut and the color of the scrubs, but he looked tanned and fit, and his shoulders seemed broader than ever. Nancy Ferguson sat beside him, laughing at something he was saying.

"They weren't together last night," Sybil remarked, looking their way.

Claire glanced back at her breakfast partner. Though she hated to perpetuate the gossip mill, she couldn't help asking, "How do you know?"

"Robbie was awake after the unit meeting. He wanted me to stay and watch a movie with him. I don't ordinarily play Peeping Tom, but I happened to notice her leaving the building, and I also happened to notice Dr. Brady going to his office."

"He could have left later," Claire pointed out.

"He didn't. The floor nurse told me he planned to sleep in his office. He wanted to be in X ray early with Meghan."

Claire glanced back across the cafeteria. The red-haired nurse had placed her hand on his arm. Jack listened intently to whatever she was telling him. "I met her yesterday," Claire said. "She's a very nice person."

"Yes, she is," Sybil agreed. "And she's a great nurse, too. But that doesn't mean she should get the hero."

Claire smiled. "You're jaded, Sybil."

"Realistic."

"I don't want him."

The other woman arched a disbelieving eyebrow. "Really? Then why are you upset?"

It was a good question. Unfortunately Claire didn't have an answer, nor did she have a reply for the little voice that nagged at her, telling her it knew that she was lying. The problem with having come here was that she wanted Jack terribly. She loved him desperately, and she always had. She just had to keep herself from depending on him.

Sybil grinned at her. "You know, Claire, far be it for me to contradict you, but you don't seem to be as unconcerned as you claim to be."

Claire studied the woman across from her. "I like you, too."

Sybil laughed.

A few moments later Nancy left the cafeteria. Next, the group of doctors stood to leave. Claire watched Jack head toward the exit. He was almost out of the door when he happened to look back and see her. Caught unaware, he stared at her with undisguised longing in his eyes. She met his gaze, then deliberately looked away. She didn't want to lead him on.

But he excused himself, waving the others on and heading back inside the cafeteria toward her. Just watching him walk across the room accelerated her heart rate into overdrive. No, she certainly wasn't unconcerned.

"Good morning." He paused by their table. Although he acknowledged both women, his smile was for Claire. "Sleep well?"

Up close the scrubs fit him more nicely than from across the room and he looked awfully fresh for someone who had slept on a sofa. She was awfully impressed for someone who didn't care. "Yes, thank you."

He glanced down at her plate. "And you ate a good breakfast?"

"Not good," she answered. "But I ate it." The eggs had tasted even worse than they'd looked.

He laughed. "Hospital food does lack that certain something. Have you seen Meghan yet?"

Claire shook her head. "No. Did she do all right this morning?"

"Fine. Considering all she's been through, she's a good little sport. By the way, why didn't you tell me you were Meghan's blood type?"

"I didn't know it," Claire answered.

"We got the results this morning. You're a good match."

Claire was surprised. Meghan looked so much like Jack, Claire had thought her child his clone. For some reason it made her happy to realize she was her daughter's blood type. "Do you have any other results?"

"We have a bit to wait, yet. She just had X rays early this morning. Going up? I'll walk you."

No, the little voice screamed. *The man is dangerous. You don't want to be with him.* Yet she could hardly refuse; she did want to see her daughter, and she was finished eating. She had to accept the fact that she was going to be with Jack constantly, whether she liked it or not. He was not a threat, she told herself.

Sure, and the universe was inhabited by little green men.

If only he weren't so attractive. If only she hadn't fallen in love with him all those years ago.

She glanced at Sybil for help, but the other woman suddenly decided she needed another cup of coffee. "You guys go ahead," she drawled. "I'm going to have one more mug of caffeine. Gotta get through the day, you know."

"Caffeine's no good for you," Jack told her.

"Don't give me a lecture, Doc. It's my only vice and I'm keeping it. See you later."

He smiled with that thousand-watt grin of his. No wonder he was so charismatic, Claire thought. He could charm a snake away from a snake charmer just by grinning. "You'll regret it this afternoon when you get heartburn."

"We'll see." Sybil stuck out her tongue in defiance.

"Ready?" Jack held out his hand for Claire.

She didn't have much choice. While Sybil headed for the coffee machine, Claire left the cafeteria with him. They walked down the hall, headed toward the elevator.

"How was the movie last night?" She didn't know what else to talk about—she could hardly tell him her heart was racing just being near him—and she did wonder if what Sybil had told her was in fact true.

He shrugged. "I didn't get to watch it. I had some charts to go over."

He sounded so casual. His reply was not exactly confirmation, but she noticed he didn't mention Nancy. "Maybe you can catch it another night."

"Maybe. Did you get to go out shopping yet?"

"No."

"Good. Don't. I hope you don't mind, but I called a department store and had a coat sent over this morning. It's in Meghan's room."

She glanced at him. Why was she surprised? Jack had always been thoughtful—absent but thoughtful. "Thank you."

"You're welcome. I hope you like it. It's red down. I figured since you had to put up with all the snow you might do better in a cheerful color. There are mittens and a scarf, too."

"No hat?"

"I thought you didn't like hats."

"I don't, but the way Sybil talks, you don't allow any-one to do anything around here that might jeopardize their health. Didn't you always use to tell me that I lost most of my body heat through my head?"

"I also told you not to worry about it, that I'd keep you warm," he answered softly.

Claire realized that the problem with the past was that it could come back to haunt you. He'd told her that just before he'd made love to her one night. She'd com-plained about the lack of heat in their apartment. Since there wasn't anything he could do, he'd produced a stocking cap and pulled it over her head, telling her she needed to wear it wherever she went. Then he'd decided that as long as they were home, that was the *only* item of clothing she should wear. One thing had led to another and pretty soon she wasn't cold at all. They'd spent the night keeping each other warm.

They had arrived at the elevator. Not wanting to ac-knowledge that particular incident, Claire looked around at the paintings on the wall, pretending she'd never seen them before. They were from a local art gallery, and ac-cording to the small piece of paper tucked in the corner sporting a price tag, any sale benefited the hospital guild.

Although she imagined his memory of that night was as vivid as hers, thankfully Jack didn't press the subject. He shoved his hands into his pockets and glanced at the paintings, too.

"Claire, we need to talk."

He dropped the words in a low, quiet voice. So he wasn't leaving it alone, after all. She glanced at him.

Couldn't he take no for an answer? "We are talking."

He shook his head. "No, not like this. I'd like to clear up what happened between us, once and for all."

She sighed. "Jack, I keep telling you there's nothing to clear up."

"And I told you last night you were lying. There is something between us, whether you like it or not. I'd like for us to acknowledge it."

"And then what?"

"We'll deal with it."

That was the last thing she needed. "No. I've told you, I can't go back to that pain."

"There's pain?"

What was he getting at? Of course she'd been hurt. "A great deal."

"Then there has to be caring," he said. "You wouldn't hurt if you didn't care."

Where on earth had he come up with that one? "Jack, you're twisting things so they fit your own meaning. Please don't turn my words around."

"Do you care?"

"I've told you over and over how I feel."

"No, you haven't," he corrected. "You've told me once. Even doctors allow for a second opinion."

"Jack—" She glanced around at the crowd of people that had joined them waiting for the elevator. She hated having her personal life on display, like the paintings, bandied about freely. "I'm sorry, but this isn't the time or the place to discuss our relationship."

"No, it isn't," he agreed. "I'll see you tonight. We'll go to dinner across the street."

Claire opened her mouth to protest, but right then the elevator doors slid open; the car was already packed with people. Unless they wanted to miss it, they had to get on. She certainly didn't want to talk anymore. As they squeezed inside, Jack nodded and murmured hello to practically everyone. Since the car was crowded, it seemed natural for him to place his arm around her shoulders in a protective gesture. Uncomfortable but unable to move away, Claire stood close to him until they got off on the fourth floor. Once there, she managed to pull back, walking quickly so he couldn't guide her or touch her.

She didn't have to worry about being near him any longer, though. The moment they stepped out of the elevator, he was bombarded at every turn by someone wanting to speak to him—doctors, nurses, patients. It took half an hour for them to make their way down the hall. At one point Claire started to go by herself, but he signaled to her to stay. She stood against the wall, waiting for him.

"Sorry," he said when he caught up with her.

"A problem with a patient?"

"Patients," he clarified. "Just minor."

"What's *major*, Jack?"

He could hardly miss her point. "Claire, it doesn't have to be this way."

She shook her head in despair. "It always was."

Then she entered Meghan's room, and Claire saw that her daughter looked better than she had in several days. The child was sitting up in bed laughing. Only she held a brand-new teddy bear clutched in her arms and she was laughing with Jack's mother. When Claire walked in, she wanted to turn around and walk back out. Although she'd known that Mrs. Brady was coming to visit, she hadn't thought it would be this soon, and certainly not right after she'd had an emotional encounter with Jack.

Angeline Brady was a tall woman, thin and striking, just like her son and granddaughter. In fact, looking at Jack, Meghan and his mother was like staring at mirror images, except Mrs. Brady had a good deal of gray running through her dark hair. For some reason she had always intimidated Claire, and today was no exception. Seeing Meghan with the fuzzy brown teddy bear made Claire bristle with animosity—as well as immediate guilt. How could the woman know what the stuffed animal represented to Claire? They hadn't talked in years.

"Well, good morning," Jack said, going to his mother's side and hugging her. "You're out early."

"Yes." She turned to Claire. The smile on her face was genuine. So was the look of hesitation. Clearly she wasn't sure of her welcome. "Hello, Claire," she murmured softly. "How are you?"

"Fine."

"You look wonderful."

"Thank you."

"So does Meghan. She's a beautiful child. You've done a lovely job raising her."

Claire acknowledged the compliment with a smile. "Thanks," she said again, still feeling uneasy. The least she could do was be polite. "I hear you've had a grandson at last."

The woman beamed. "Markie's going to be a doctor."

"I'm going to be a lawyer," Meghan piped up.

"Really?" Mrs. Brady turned back to her granddaughter with a look of pride. "A doctor and a lawyer in the same family. Why, Grandpa and I will have nothing to worry about."

Kathleen must have thought it all a bore. The young teenager glanced drolly at the four of them. "I'm going to be a soap-opera star." She smiled at Jack and popped a bubble. "What do you think, Dr. Brady? Do you think they'll like me on *Great Hospital*?"

Jack grinned back. "I think they'll love you, Kathy, gum and all." A page calling him to the telephone cut into the conversation. "I'd better go," he said. "I've still got to make rounds. I'll see you all later. Don't forget the jacket, Claire. It's in the box by the bed."

She thought he might forget their date, but then he said, "See you tonight. Six o'clock."

"Wait, Jack," his mother called as he swept out the door and down the hall. "When are you coming for dinner?"

"Soon."

"Sunday," she said. "I'll fix a roast Sunday! You come." When he was gone she turned to Claire. "Do you think he'll show up?"

Claire shrugged. "I don't know."

"I can't help worrying about him."

"He's busy." Odd how she was defending him.

"Yes, he is," his mother answered. "Too busy. Well—" she gave another nervous smile "—I guess I'd better go, too. I have some errands to run. I'll come back to visit Meghan tomorrow if it's all right with you."

"It's fine. Come anytime."

After kissing Meghan and saying goodbye, Mrs. Brady walked toward the door. All of a sudden she paused and turned back. "Claire?"

"Yes?"

The woman looked increasingly uncomfortable. "Would you walk me to the elevator? There's something I wanted to talk to you about."

Claire was puzzled by the request. She glanced at Meghan and Kathleen, but both girls were absorbed in a rock video that had come on television. There was no excuse not to go. "Sure."

"Thank you."

Jack's mother acted even more hesitantly as they walked together down the hallway. Claire couldn't help but wonder what was going on in her mind. They got halfway to the elevator before his mother sighed and said, "I meant what I told you earlier about Meghan. You've done a good job with her, Claire. She's a delightful child. And I'm sorry."

Claire frowned. "About what?"

"For not supporting you when you were married to Jack. I was wrong, and I deeply regret it."

"Mrs. Brady, my problems with Jack had nothing to do with you. It's not your fault my marriage failed," she said gently.

The woman's expression was sad. She obviously disagreed. "It may not be my fault, but I didn't make things any easier on you. In fact, if I were to admit the truth, I'd have to tell you that I wanted to drive you away. I knew if I ignored you, you would get lonely and leave."

"But why?" Claire was amazed at such a revelation. "Why would you want to do such a thing?"

"Jack is my youngest child, my baby. I didn't want to share him." Her smile was apologetic, bittersweet, and she sighed heavily, as if she were hurting inside. "I know, it was selfish of me. I realize that now. Actually, I realized it when you left, and Jack was so destroyed. But we do foolish things, Claire, we mothers. I'm sure you can understand that, now that you have your own child."

Claire could easily understand. She had done many things in the name of motherhood of which she wasn't exactly proud—yelling at the little boy next door who'd hurt Meghan, defending her child when Meghan had been wrong, not disciplining Meghan properly. But she frowned at his mother, puzzled. "Why are you telling me this now?"

"Because I swore that if you let me come here today and see my granddaughter I'd admit the truth and try to make it up to you." They paused in front of the elevator doors. Mrs. Brady looked at Claire with a pleading expression in her eyes. "Can you please find it in your heart to forgive me? I'm a foolish woman and the only excuse I can offer is that I love my son. Now I know that what I did was wrong, and I want to see him happy."

For all her harbored resentment, Claire found it hard to dislike someone who begged forgiveness. "Mrs. Brady, you don't have to apologize to me."

"Yes, I do. Please let me do that much. Don't take that away from me."

Claire nodded, knowing she would have felt the same way. "Then I accept your apology."

"Thank you." Jack's mother placed her hand on Claire's arm and squeezed, saying, "You're a lovely girl, Claire."

"Mrs. Brady, please—" She felt uncomfortable.

"I know. I'm upsetting you. I won't get maudlin again. Meghan's going to be okay, you know." She smiled. "Jack will take care of her."

Now it was Claire's turn to be grateful. Words of support were always welcome. "I hope you're right."

"Would you like to come to dinner, too, Sunday?"

"I'll think about it," Claire said, not wanting to refuse outright.

The elevator doors slid open and Mrs. Brady started to step on. "Thank you. I'll see you tomorrow?"

Claire nodded. "I'll be here."

"Then take care."

The doors closed. Claire turned to go back to Meghan's room, only to nearly run into Nancy Ferguson rounding the corner. For a moment the two women paused and animosity flashed in the green eyes of the nurse. But then she smiled. "Good morning," she said. "Feeling better?"

"Yes, thank you." Claire was being so polite today, she felt as if she needed a tape recording.

"How was breakfast?"

"Fine."

"I see Jack's mother was here."

Claire couldn't help but wonder what the conversation was leading up to. She wasn't certain how many emotional encounters she could take in one day. But she nodded. "Yes, she came to see Meghan."

"Good. I'm glad." The red-haired woman paused as if torn between wanting to talk, to say something, and needing to go. Apparently she decided to leave. "Let me know if you need anything."

"Sure."

Claire watched her hurry away, then turned back and noticed Jack at the nurses' station. He was talking on the telephone, with a chart in front of him and three others piled beneath it. Two nurses stood waiting to speak to him, and someone else scrawled him a note. She wondered where he got his energy, his drive and motivation. Few people could keep up his pace.

But nothing had changed. Medicine was still his first and only love. Why, then, was she still attracted to him? She sighed. If only Nancy Ferguson could give her the huge dose of resistance she needed. Except defenses had to be developed, not given to her by another person. Like it or not, she was attracted to Jack. And like it or not, she had to deal with it.

Chapter 5

Jack had also ordered a pink jacket with matching gloves, hat and scarf for Meghan. When Claire got back to the room and opened the boxes, she was stunned by all the clothing. How had he known their sizes, tastes? And how had he gotten everything so quickly? Like most children, her daughter was delighted with the surprise, especially with the soft, puffy jacket. Despite the intravenous solution still dripping into her arm, Meghan wanted to try everything on. First she modeled, draping the coat over her shoulders and preening in bed, mittens and all, then Claire slipped her own outfit on.

Kathleen, who was part of the snowbelt area of Ohio, stated that she couldn't understand the fuss over something as mundane as winter clothes. So what if they'd be warm? A coat was a coat. Now a Navy pea jacket or an army fatigue jacket, that was a different story. A cashmere sweater might be nice, too—something in the latest fashion. Boots were gauche, even fur-lined suede. Nobody who expected to be anybody wore them.

But Meghan liked her boots best of all. Claire thought they were pretty special, too. They were so attractive and would be great if she wanted to go shopping or walk back and forth to the dorm.

When Jack stopped by later, they had to model everything all over again.

"Is it cold out?" Meghan asked her father as she draped the scarf around her neck until it nearly covered her face. Her two stuffed animals were propped in her bed, one beside the other.

"I think the temperature this morning was ten below zero. Why?"

"Is that cold?"

Jack laughed and ruffled her hair. "Yes, it's cold."

What an understatement, Claire thought with a shiver as Meghan answered, "Good. I want it to be cold."

"But why?" he asked again, frowning.

"So I can wear my coat when I go home from the hospital," she answered logically.

"Good idea."

Odd how children reasoned—they didn't have a home here, yet Meghan, who was sick, still anticipated going home.

"Will you wear your coat, Mommy?"

"Absolutely," Claire answered. "In fact, I think I'm going to wear it right now. I need to run over to the dorm to call Grandma Warren." She glanced at Jack. "Is it okay for me to leave for a few minutes? The fresh air will do me good."

"Sure, but why are you calling your mother from there?"

Claire shrugged. "It's cheaper than using the phone here." Although Jack had been generous with child support, she had refused alimony and consequently she'd never stopped pinching pennies. Perhaps it was the influence of living with her mother. They were a frugal pair, especially after Claire's father had died when she'd been a child. "I promised I'd call at noon today."

Jack sighed. "Look, Claire, you don't have to go to the dorm to call your mother. I'll be glad to pay the phone bill from here. I can afford it, no matter where you want to place the call. Feel free to use any phone in the hospital. Just tell them to bill the charges to me."

She gave him a polite smile. "That's nice of you, Jack, but I don't expect you to do that."

"I'm not doing it because you expect it," he answered firmly. "I'd *like* to do it. So, please, don't argue. How much are you saving, anyhow? Two cents a minute?" He nodded to the phone. "Call your mother."

He was being presumptuous again, telling her what to do. Yet he made sense. Sometimes she spent ten cents to save one, and she didn't really want to leave Meghan. "What if I had wanted an excuse to wear the jacket?"

"Weird," Kathleen remarked, but she was watching television so it was hard to figure out what she was referring to.

"Yeah," Meghan agreed.

Jack smiled, arching an eyebrow at the girls. "We were married once, remember?" he said, turning back to Claire. "I know you, and I doubt you're all that anxious to dress in down."

For some reason she blushed, embarrassed by his reminder of her behavior all those years ago. This was the first time he'd ever alluded to it. "Point taken."

"Claire, I didn't mean to insult you."

She shook her head. What was the sense of getting into an argument? "You didn't." She unclipped her earring and went to the phone. "Shall I tell Mother you said hello?"

"Please do." He bent to kiss Meghan. "I'll see you later, honey. Send Mommy for lunch as soon as she's off the phone."

The man obviously had a fetish about meals. First he'd insisted she eat breakfast, then he'd invited her to dinner, now he wanted her to go for lunch.

Meghan smiled. "See you later?"

"You betcha."

Although she was busy dialing the number, Claire watched as he left the room. He was still so tall and darkly handsome. Somehow life just wasn't fair, and these days it was dealing her a stacked deck.

Her mother must have been waiting beside the phone. Annabelle Warren answered on the first ring. Claire turned her attention back to her mother. She chatted for a while and then let Meghan talk. Since Jack didn't have any test results back yet, there wasn't much to report, except that it was cold and snowy, which still excited her daughter. To the child the snow was like a gift from heaven.

After they hung up, Kathleen went for occupational therapy and Meghan fell asleep. Claire left for lunch, but she didn't know anyone in the cafeteria. She sat by herself and munched on an apple, thinking about the old adage and wishing it were true. If an apple a day kept the doctor away she'd eat a ton of them for her daughter's sake and a semitruckful for Kathleen and all the other patients. And another bushel for herself, she thought. She surely needed to keep the doctor away—one doctor in particular.

With a sigh she started back upstairs. Unfortunately, eating wouldn't help and neither would going out with Jack tonight. How was she going to deal with him? He reminded her of things best forgotten—things once forgotten. If she continued seeing him, she'd soon remember just the good times and not the bad. Maybe the apple wouldn't keep the doctor away, but it had tempted the serpent in the Garden of Eden. Claire sighed. She needed to get a better perspective on the situation. No, she *needed* to cancel dinner.

As it turned out she didn't have to cancel because Jack did. At six o'clock a nurse rushed into Meghan's room just as Claire was getting ready to find Jack and tell him she had other things to do. "Mrs. Brady, I'm glad I caught you," the nurse said a bit breathlessly. "Dr. Brady just called and wanted me to tell you that he's tied up. He's not going to be able to have dinner tonight."

Claire paused. "He's not?"

"No. He's over at Memorial on a consultation."

"I see." She didn't know whether to be angry or relieved. She didn't want to be alone with Jack, and even though she had intended to find a way to get out of seeing him, it irritated her that nothing had changed. He was still canceling engagements at the last minute. In a way, however, it vindicated her. This was something she'd put up with since the day they'd met. "Thank you."

The nurse smiled. "He said he still needed to talk to you, but to go ahead and have dinner without him."

Claire nodded. "I will."

"He's such a busy man," the nurse went on. "I don't know where he gets his energy."

"Neither do I."

"Well, I have to go. It's time for meds. Can I do anything else for you?"

"Do you have any test results on Meghan yet?"

The nurse shook her head. "Sorry, nothing. It takes a couple of days. We should be getting something soon, though."

"I guess I'll just have wait."

"I know it's hard waiting. Have a good night, Mrs. Brady."

That would be an impossibility until her daughter was well, but Claire was glad for the support. "Thanks. Would you mind if I went on over to Care House? I'm still tired, and Meghan's making potholders."

The ladies from Occupational Therapy had visited and given the child oodles of fabric loops that went on a frame. Meghan had decided to make presents for her grandparents. The nurse glanced into the room at the dark-haired little girl so diligently placing strips on tiny plastic nails, and nodded. "Sure, we'll take care of her. You go ahead and get some rest."

"If you need me I'll be in my room."

"No problem. I might even have some time later to help her weave. The place should quiet down soon. It's almost bedtime."

After kissing her daughter, who was preoccupied with the bright strips, and checking on Sybil, who wanted to stay and chat with Robbie, Claire left for the dormitory. If nothing else, this would be a good time to shower and shampoo her hair. She still needed to straighten up her room. Sybil had helped by hanging her clothes up this morning, but her toiletries were strewn all over the place. She would get settled in, then go to bed. She hadn't been exaggerating: she was exhausted.

The shower was wonderful, warm and inviting. So were the nachos and cheese she heated in the microwave in the small kitchen down the hall. When she'd checked in at the desk yesterday, the clerk in charge had told her no one worried about convention, to just relax and enjoy the place. She could run around in her robe and slippers and no one would mind. The food was for anyone who wanted it, paid for by small donations everyone would leave. She put five dollars in the kitty and went back to her room, planning to eat, dry her hair and then fall into bed.

Claire closed her door only to open it seconds later when someone knocked. She expected Sybil but Jack stood in the doorway smiling at her, his face chapped from the cold and his hair tousled by the wind. A few snowflakes clung to the dark strands, melting now in the warmth of the dorm. He was the last person she'd expected to see.

"Hi." He glanced down at the platter of chips in her hand. "Sorry I'm late. Smells good. Is there enough for two?"

Claire stared at him for a long moment, not knowing what to say. Every time she saw him he looked taller, more masculine, and so damned sexy it ought to be against the law. Even the snowflakes looked good in his hair.

"I—no," she answered at last. "There's not enough for two. What are you doing here, Jack?"

He seemed confused by her angry tone. He glanced at her and frowned. "I left a message for you. Didn't you get it?"

"All I heard was that you weren't going to get back in time for dinner." She knew she was being difficult. As usual, he thought he could just stroll in any old time he wished and she would drop everything to be with him. "I'm busy, Jack."

"Doing what? I said I'd see you later. We still have to talk, Claire."

"I didn't think you'd come here."

"Now that I have, may I come in?"

It would be rude to refuse. Besides, her voice must have been louder than she thought. A couple of room doors opened down the hall and a few people glanced out. All Claire had on was a robe and slippers and a towel draped around her head, but she opened the door wider, letting him in.

"What is it that you want to talk about?" she asked as she went to set the nacho platter on the night table. "I told you this morning I don't have anything more to say."

He had closed the door behind him and taken off his coat. He tossed it on the chair. "But I do."

"What is it?" Now that her hands were free she tucked her robe more tightly around her waist.

He followed her motions. "Don't worry, I'm not going to force you."

"I didn't think you would."

"Really?" He glanced pointedly at her hands. "Claire, why is it that you don't want to see me?"

Because I don't want to be alone with you. Because no matter what happened between us, I still care for you. Because you wouldn't have to force me. All you'd have to do is touch me, be near me, and I'd fall at your feet. Not wise to admit all that. "Because there's no reason to see you."

"I'm sorry, but I disagree. Whether you care to acknowledge it or not, there's something between us."

"Yes," she admitted. "I agree. There is something between us. We share a child."

"Who proves we were once in love," he said.

Didn't he ever give up? "The key word there is *once*, Jack," she said. "We're not kids anymore. I tried to make it very clear yesterday that the only reason I came here was because of our daughter. What do you want from me?"

"I want the truth."

She shook her head in disagreement. "No, you don't. You want me to say that I love you. I don't know what you think you're going to gain from it. So what if I did? What would it prove?"

"I'd know how you feel about me."

"But what would it prove?"

He didn't answer right away. When he did, his tone was guarded. She could almost feel his pain, the depth of his need. "You may not believe this, Claire, but if I knew how you felt, I'd know whether or not to fight for you."

She sighed heavily. She had to make things crystal clear to him. "Jack, even if I did love you, it wouldn't do any good for you to fight for me. Our marriage is over. It was over a long time ago. No matter what we do, we can't bring it back. Maybe it's my fault, but I can't be second best. I can't take a back seat to medicine. I never could."

"I could try to make medicine second best."

Surely he wasn't serious. She shoved her hands into her pockets and shook her head in disbelief. "Good Lord, Jack, how can you say that after you canceled dinner to-night?"

"Tonight was an exception."

She nearly laughed. "That's my exact point. With you, every night's an exception; every case, every patient, every symptom, every disease. I don't want to feel jealous of a sick person. I don't want to wait night after night for you to come home, resenting the life you're saving. I don't want to share you with anyone or anything. Maybe that's selfish and shallow of me, and if it is, I'm sorry, but I want a normal relationship based on love and caring and sharing and being together.''

"I can give you that, Claire."

"Jack, please, be realistic. This is your life." She gestured toward the hospital. "You love it. You're good at it, and you should have a woman who understands that and wants you anyhow." Although she felt shallow admitting it, she had to tell the truth. "Unfortunately, I don't."

"You could try."

"I don't want to do that, either."

"Why not?"

"It wouldn't work."

"Even though we care for each other?" Slowly, deliberately, he moved toward her, closing the gap between them. A shiver snaked down her spine. When he was directly in front of her, he tilted her chin up and bent his head to kiss her. "Even though we have this?"

"Jack—"

"I told you, Claire, I won't force you."

The moment his lips met hers she realized all over again why she was afraid of him. He made her feel so weak willed and vulnerable. His hands caressed her back; his mouth was soft and tender on hers.

"How can you deny it?" he asked huskily, drawing away to trace his finger along her lips. "How can you pretend it doesn't exist?"

She wished she had an answer to his questions. "Jack, I told you the other day that sex doesn't prove anything. It doesn't prove anything tonight, either. So we're attracted to each other. So what? It's physical." She pulled away.

"I think you're wrong—or at least *my* feelings are more than physical. But I won't press you anymore." Turning away, he picked up his coat. "I'd better go." Just before he walked out the door, he paused. "I'll be around if you need me. Just say the word, Claire."

She was surprised at his sudden change of attitude. Was he trying to trick her with a new tactic, wanting her to make the first move. "I'm sorry, Jack."

He smiled. "Hey, I'm a big boy. I can take it. See you later, okay?"

He closed the door behind him with a soft click. Claire stared at the empty space for a long time. Then she turned to the bed.

Claire wanted to be at the unit early enough to eat breakfast with Meghan. She hadn't slept much last night. After Jack had left, she'd gone to bed, but she'd tossed and turned and rested very little. When her alarm went off, she got up and pulled on her clothes and headed across the walkway. No matter what happened, she would spend today with her daughter.

She was almost there when a nurse called to her. "Oh, Mrs. Brady, Dr. Brady wants to see you if you've got a minute. I was just trying to call you at Care House."

Claire's first thought was of her daughter, but the nurse's tone wasn't urgent, so surely everything was all right. Perhaps Jack had changed his mind and he wanted to see her to press her about their relationship. "Is he in his office?"

The nurse smiled and said, "Isn't he always? There or with a patient. I keep telling him that he uses the shower here more than the patients. Just knock. By the way, I think Meghan's still asleep. I'll let you know if she wakes up."

"Thanks."

Jack wasn't alone in his office. Claire had never been introduced to the short, stocky man sitting in the chair across the desk from her ex-husband, but somehow she knew he was Dr. Hal Davies, the physician in charge of her daughter's case. Her heart hit the floor. The moment she opened the door to the room she knew that, contrary to the nurse's attitude, this was serious business. It was about Meghan and it wasn't good.

But that was silly, she told herself. She was overreacting again. She clenched her hands at her sides and took a deep breath, hoping she was right.

Yet knowing she was wrong.

She tried to sound cheery as she stepped into the room and closed the door behind her. "You wanted to see me? I was just on my way to eat breakfast with Meghan. I didn't want to miss another great meal."

Jack sat at his desk, looking as solemn as she felt. "Come on in, Claire," he said quietly. "We need to talk to you."

Her heart hammered with fear as she settled on the edge of the same chair she'd occupied two days ago and stared at her ex-husband. Both men looked so serious. Too serious. "What's wrong, Jack?" she asked, although she knew. "You've got Meghan's test results, right?"

"Claire—" He started to speak, but his voice choked. At that point the other man leaned over and held out his hand.

"Mrs. Brady, I'm Hal Davies, the doctor in charge of Meghan's case."

Up close, Hal Davies was taller than Claire had at first thought, with sandy hair and a ruddy complexion. Like Jack, he wore a white lab coat with a stethoscope tucked in his pocket. A small gold name tag proclaimed his status as a physician. She inclined her head. "It's nice to meet you."

"Yes," he returned politely. "Very nice. Mrs. Brady, Jack and I have been going over the chart and reviewing Meghan's test results."

"You have everything?"

"We just got the results from X ray this morning and her lab work is all in."

"And?" Claire asked when he paused.

He seemed uncomfortable. "I guess there's no sense in hedging. I've got some bad news, and I may as well tell you right out. Jack already knows. Meghan has advanced kidney disease. There's nothing that can be done medically to help her."

Claire sat very still, listening to the low, grave words. She'd tried to prepare herself for this moment. She'd thought about it, dreaded it, rehearsed it, denied it, hated it, postponed it; and yet she still couldn't accept it. Not Meghan, not her baby.

"I'm sorry, Mrs. Brady. I know this is disappointing news."

What a strange word, *disappointing*. A person was disappointed when a job didn't come through or when a dress didn't fit or when a dinner burned. Sometimes even a relationship might be disappointing. But this wasn't disappointing—this was totally devastating. She felt destroyed by the words. She just sat staring at him.

"But can't you—" She touched her forehead, trying to think, trying to hold back the panic clutching her gut. "Nothing? Nothing can be done to help her?"

"Nothing medically," Hal Davies answered. "No pills, no medication. There is nothing that will work. Her kidneys have almost totally shut down. I'm afraid we can't reverse the process. I'm so sorry."

She felt as if her heart—her soul—had been ripped out of her body. This was her child, her flesh and blood. "But why? What had happened? How did it start? Why Meghan?"

"We don't know. If we had the answer to that, we'd have a cure. Unfortunately we have no idea why some people develop kidney disease and others don't. All we can do is hope for the best."

Claire hated platitudes. At least Jack had never pulled any punches with her. She glanced at him. He was as distraught as she was, perhaps more so. He sat in the chair totally stunned, staring at the green blotter that covered his desk. He hadn't been prepared, either—even though he was a doctor, even though he'd been privy to her chart. How odd, Claire thought. He'd been pretending, too. How she wished she could deny this one. All she had to do was turn around and go back out the door, pretend they hadn't called to her. Why had she let down her guard in the first place? Every other time she'd looked at Jack or talked to him or even heard from him, she had steeled herself for this moment.

"What can be done?" Claire asked finally. "What about a transplant? Can she get a kidney? Would that help her?"

Dr. Davies nodded. "Yes. It would help a great deal."

Claire actually smiled. There was hope, after all. Why were they so forlorn? "Then let's do it. Immediately. The more time we wait the worse she'll get, right? I can have surgery tomorrow—this morning, if necessary."

Hal Davies drew a deep breath. "It's not that simple, Mrs. Brady. We have a bit of a problem there, too."

"What do you mean?" Claire was confused. "What problem? I'm Meghan's mother. Jack told me just yesterday morning that we were the same blood type. I can give her a kidney. Does she need two?"

"Even if we could, we wouldn't take both of your kidneys," the doctor told her. "You need one to live, you know."

She nodded agreement. She was just being overanxious. "I understand that. But what do we have to do? Do you want me to sign some papers? Take some tests? What?"

"Nothing just yet," Hal Davies answered. "As I mentioned before, we have a bit of a complication."

"What are you trying to say?" Although Claire realized he was trying to be gentle, to lead her through everything carefully, she wanted him to get to the point. "Look, I'll go for counseling," she went on, remembering the things Sybil had mentioned. "I'll be glad to talk to the psychiatrist. I'll do anything."

"Including risking your own life?" Jack asked.

It was the first time he'd spoken and Claire glared at him. Pain was etched in every feature of his face. "How much of a risk can it be?" she asked. "You're just going to take out my kidney, right? Minor surgery."

"It's *major* surgery, Claire, which is always dangerous." He got up and paced across the room, staring out the window just as she had a couple of days ago. She had a feeling he wasn't really seeing anything, either. "Anytime we administer anesthesia and drugs, we run the risk of death."

"Don't try to scare me, Jack. People have surgery every day."

He turned back to her. "Not when they have a bleeding problem."

She frowned. "I have a bleeding problem?"

He nodded and returned to his desk, flopping defeated in his chair. "Don't you remember when you delivered Meghan? You almost bled to death."

"But I was fine afterward," she said, not understanding. "They stopped the bleeding."

"Claire, I don't think you realized how close to death you came." Jack's expression was still somber, concerned. "I didn't. Not until I checked your old charts on microfilm. You have a blood dyscrasia, a clotting disorder. It's minor, but it's there."

"That's impossible." She shook her head. "Someone would have told me."

"I don't know why you weren't told," he answered. "I don't know why I wasn't told. You should have been warned in case you had more children or needed surgery. At the very least you should be on vitamins."

Vitamins. They were discussing her daughter's life and he was concerned about vitamins.

"Haven't you ever had dental work, Mrs. Brady?" Dr. Davies cut in.

Claire glanced at him. "I get my teeth cleaned all the time."

Although he obviously realized she was being facetious, he wasn't angry. "I meant, did you ever have a tooth pulled?"

"No."

"Nothing since you had Meghan?" Jack kept probing. "No dental work? No minor surgeries? Cuts that needed stitches?"

She bruised easily but Claire shook her head. "Nothing. I'm fine. Really, I'm very healthy. I'm telling you I can do this." She glanced from one to the other. "I can give Meghan my kidney."

Hal Davies just frowned at her. "Mrs. Brady, it's awfully risky."

"Maybe," she agreed, shrugging. "But what are the alternatives?"

Jack was the one who answered. "We can put Meghan on the list for a donor organ. She's young. We can start dialysis right away."

"And she'll have to wait, right?" Like Sybil and Robbie. Like so many other patients. Wait and hope.

Jack nodded. "Yes."

"She'll get sicker."

"A person can live for a long time on dialysis these days," Jack said.

"But a kidney is better."

"Yes."

She thought for a long moment. She wasn't about to quit now. "Jack, does this blood dyscrasia affect my kidneys in any way?"

"No. Why?"

"They function normally, right?"

"I'd have to have some tests run to determine that with any degree of certainty, but generally a blood dyscrasia doesn't have anything to do with kidney function. Why?"

"And Meghan couldn't get the blood dyscrasia from me? She couldn't catch it, right?"

"A blood dyscrasia isn't communicable, Claire. What are you getting at?"

She would have to go carefully to make them see reason. She realized that as doctors they had an obligation to her, too; yet Meghan was the most important thing in her life. "Jack, what would you do if I needed surgery? What would you do if I had appendicitis and you needed to operate?"

"You don't have appendicitis, Claire."

"But what would you do if I did have it?" she kept asking. "If you were the doctor, what would you do?"

He shrugged. "I'd have to operate, of course."

"And how would you treat my blood dyscrasia?"

"I'd give you medication to help your blood clot."

"And if I hemorrhaged?"

"I'd give you blood." He sighed, obviously realizing what she was getting at. "Claire, there's a terrible risk of blood-transmitted diseases these days."

"But I could also die from the anesthesia or a complication of surgery, a blood clot or pneumonia. It's a risk I'd have to take. But if I needed surgery, you'd have to do it."

"Yes," he agreed.

"Then I don't see why you can't take my kidney," she concluded. "As far as I'm concerned, I have to have surgery. This is an emergency."

"Claire, you don't understand."

"No," she countered. "You don't understand. This is my child and I'd do *anything* to help her." She choked back tears. "Please, Jack, I have to do this."

"You could die."

"I could die anytime."

"I don't buy that one. I never have. The odds of walking across the street and getting hit by a car aren't anywhere near the same as lying on a table and donating your kidney."

"Jack, if you were Meghan's blood type would you give her your kidney?" When he hesitated she pressed, "Would you?"

"Yes."

"I'm her blood type."

"Claire, what if you die?"

"Then Meghan will live through me," she said softly. "She'll have my life."

"Claire—"

"This is what I want, Jack. Can't you understand that? Please don't be the doctor today," she went on pleading, her voice a mere whisper. "Please understand. Please help me find a way to help our child. Just today—please . . . please be her father."

Chapter 6

For the next several days Claire didn't even think about her relationship with Jack. Her entire life was taken up with caring for Meghan and preparing for surgery. Jack was beside her constantly, supporting her through a barrage of tests and studies and consultations. She was poked at, proded and jabbed, and then afterward, she answered enough questions to have constituted a government survey instead of an interview for an operation. At one point she was certain she'd figured out why Sybil had put the square peg in the round hole, and Sybil wasn't even donating a kidney.

In the end the doctors came to the same conclusion Claire had reached the morning she had discovered that her daughter needed a transplant: she had a blood dyscrasia, but it wasn't anything that couldn't be treated. Therefore she could donate her kidney whenever she wished to whomever she wished and in whatever manner she wished—as long as she was apprised of the ramifications.

But now that the moment had arrived she was a little nervous. She'd just been shaved from practically head to toe, and someone had taken another vial of blood to the laboratory to add to the gallons they had already collected. According to the nurse, everything was set. Claire would be going down to the operating room first, her daughter would follow. The surgeries would be conducted in side-by-side suites and the kidney would be transplanted immediately.

Jack came to her room just after she signed the permission forms. Since she wasn't really a kidney patient she had been admitted to another floor, and she hadn't seen much of Meghan in the last few days.

"I thought I'd let you know that you're on the schedule for eight tomorrow morning," he said to her after the nurse left the room. "Hal will do the actual operation, but I'll be there to help if he needs me. You know, you'll be a little sore afterward."

"A little?"

He smiled. "Okay, a lot." Then he paused. "Claire, are you sure you want to do this?" It was the first time he'd questioned her since that morning in his office, and he took her hand in his. A casual gesture, yet supportive and increasingly disturbing. All week he'd touched her, helped her hold herself together, and she'd tried not to let him see how it affected her.

"Yes," she murmured, her voice throaty from emotion. Didn't he understand? It wasn't what she wanted; it was what she had to do. "I'm sure."

"You could bleed to death."

"I won't."

"You've been taking your medication. You haven't missed a dose?"

They'd been giving her all sorts of vitamins and other pills. "Are you kidding? You've trained your nurses well, Jack."

"All right. Good luck. I'll be pulling for you. Now—" His tone changed and he sounded cheerful. Was he trying to be deliberately optimistic? "How about a trip up to see Meghan? I thought we might weave some potholders."

"Isn't she done yet?"

He rolled his eyes in an exaggerated gesture. "Please. She's decided to make both grandmothers an entire set."

"A set of potholders?" Claire had never heard of such a thing.

"Each one is a different color." He chuckled again, shaking his head in dismay. "Do you have any idea how many colors there are in this world? I hope the occupational therapy ladies don't come up with any more strips. We'll need a semitruck for a gift box."

Claire laughed, glad that Jack had grown even closer to their child these last few days. The two of them needed more time together. "Let's just hope she doesn't decide to make hot pads. The last I heard, the loom could be changed to accommodate different sizes of fabric."

Jack's expression sobered. "Actually, she can make anything she wants," he said softly. "As long as she gets through this."

Claire had been so busy insisting she donate a kidney that she hadn't stopped to completely consider all the risks to Meghan. Suddenly she realized that this was major surgery for her daughter, too. "Jack, how much danger is there to Meghan? Could anything happen to her?"

"There's always a danger, Claire. I explained that to you the other day."

"Will Meghan be all right?" Panic flooded her tone, squeezed her chest tight. What if Meghan didn't make it through the surgery? "Jack, please don't let anything happen to her."

"I won't." He took her by the shoulders, his grip firm and reassuring. "Calm down, Claire. She'll be fine. If anything goes wrong, I'll be there."

"And you'll come see me right away? Right after surgery?"

He nodded. "Yes. I'll let you know what's going on as soon as I can, and how she's doing. Are you sure you don't want me to call your mother? It might be a good idea to have someone with you."

Claire hadn't wanted to worry her mother. "No, please don't. She'd just be upset. She couldn't make it in time if she wanted to come, anyhow. I'll call her tomorrow night."

"You won't be feeling like calling anyone tomorrow night."

Claire smiled. "You keep telling me that, and I'm going to believe you."

"You've never had surgery."

"But I've had a baby." It was the wrong thing to say, for despite the fact that he'd been with a patient and she'd almost died that night, she had forgiven him. She'd loved him desperately, and when he'd finally appeared in her room they'd shared a moment so special she wasn't sure it could ever be duplicated. She hadn't expected to have such deep feelings about her child or about the man who had fathered that child. The love she had felt that night had been so strong and sweet that it was almost unfathomable.

"I know," he answered, and she realized he was thinking of the same moment. "I remember."

She managed a bright smile. "I'll be fine, Jack. You'll see."

"I hope so."

He reached to take her hand again, but Claire had already started down the hall. She was afraid if he touched her now she would fall apart. Or rather, into his arms. She had to hold up now more than ever. "Hope?" she chided. "In medicine? I always thought you relied more on skill and learning."

He just shrugged, falling into step beside her. "Believe me, every doctor relies on hope. Considering my specialty I probably use it more than most, but it's just as important as education. By the way, I hear my whole family's visiting Meghan tonight. Don't be surprised to see everyone. They even drove Kathleen to the solarium to watch a movie. I did make them promise not to overwhelm, Meghan though, so they won't stay long."

"Did you go for dinner today?" In all the preparations, Claire had forgotten it was Sunday. He'd been invited to his mother's.

"No, I was tied up. But she's making another roast for next Sunday. With my mother, there's always some kind of meal going on. Claire, she has always meant well."

"I know," she answered honestly. "I've recently made that discovery."

Jack slid his hands into his pockets, looking uncomfortable. "I appreciate you giving her another chance."

"I can't say it was easy, but it was the right thing to do. And we're surprisingly similar."

"A mother's love?"

She smiled. "Funny what unites people."

"Yes," he agreed, but she had a feeling they weren't discussing the same situation. "It is odd."

Jack was right about his relatives visiting. When they got upstairs, the room was filled to overflowing with his brothers, sisters, aunts, uncles. At least there weren't any little children. Meghan didn't seem in the least disturbed by all the people. She'd been dialyzed several times in preparation for surgery and she was feeling perky. She giggled and talked as though she were having a great time. When Claire and Jack walked in, all discussion stopped and everyone stared at Claire.

Uncomfortably.

Jack started to say something, but Claire knew it was up to her to put the people at ease. To her surprise, it wasn't half as difficult as she'd imagined it would be. "Good evening," she said clearly. "It's nice to see you all." She glanced at his father. "I hear the Brady name has an heir. Congratulations."

The man smiled back, his blue eyes sparkling, amused. "From a feminist like you—thanks. Want to see a picture?"

"Please."

After he pulled out a wallet with an entire string of photos of all his grandchildren, Meghan included, Jack's sister-in-law, Lucy, came to join them and they started talking, one parent to another. Soon Claire was visiting with all his relatives. She had to admit it wasn't all sweetness and light. There were a few awkward moments, like when his aunt mentioned their ill-fated marriage or when his uncle joked about the weather and Claire's aversion to snow, but she pretended everything was fine. At last everyone except her mother-in-law left. Mr. Brady had gone for the car, and Mrs. Brady stood near the door waiting for her husband and watching

Meghan swallow medication. Jack had been called out of the room and now the two women were alone.

"Before I go, I just wanted to tell you how much I admire you, Claire," Jack's mother said. "You're doing a brave thing, giving Meghan your kidney."

"It's no more than you'd do."

"Yes, but it still has to be a little frightening." Jack came back into the room just then. As though sensing Claire didn't want to talk, his mother kissed him goodnight and started for the door. "Call me tomorrow and let me know how everything goes."

"You're not coming?" he asked, puzzled.

She paused. "May I?"

"Of course," he answered. "But I'll be tied up a lot. I won't be able to wait with you."

Angeline Brady glanced at Claire. "Do you mind?"

Claire shook her head. Oddly, she didn't mind. "No. In fact, I think Meghan would like your being here."

"Then I'll see you in the morning. Thank you." She smiled again and left.

"Next you'll be invited to dinner," Jack remarked.

Claire couldn't help but chuckle. "I wouldn't go that far."

"Would you go?" he asked a few moments later.

She hadn't been prepared for that question. She thought for a minute. "You know I have a weakness for Italian food," she said finally. Actually, she had a weakness for people who needed her, and as strange as it seemed, she sensed that his mother needed her. "As long as she serves lasagna I'll be there."

Now Jack laughed. "Lasagna, huh? I'll remind her. Ready to say good-night to Meghan?"

The child had taken her medicine and was yawning sleepily. Claire bent down and brushed her lips across her daughter's cheek. "I love you, honey."

"Did you see the snowman, Mommy?"

Claire frowned. "You built a snowman?"

"Daddy 'n' me." Meghan smiled. "You can see it out the window if you want to look."

"You took her out in the cold?" Claire glanced at Jack as she went to the window.

"Just for a little bit. Don't worry, she was bundled up."

Sure enough, a huge snowman sat in the yard below them. All Meghan would have to do was glance out the window to see it.

"I stuck my tongue out and tasted a snowflake, too. Isn't it beautiful, Mommy?" the child asked.

If Claire were to tell the truth, the snowman was quite pathetic looking. It was leaning to one side, and the big part on the bottom was flat on one side. The head joined the body halfway down the shoulders. But it fit the one requirement Meghan had insisted upon: it was big.

"It's lovely," Claire said.

"I don't know." Jack joined her at the window. "We did a good job, but I think it needs something."

"A scarf," Meghan said. "Daddy wouldn't let me put mine around it. I had to stay bundled up. And a mouth. It's not smiling."

Claire nodded agreement. "A smile would probably help, but it's a lovely snowman, Meghan." She couldn't prevent the lump that formed in her throat. She was glad they had taken the time to build it. If Meghan didn't make it— She couldn't start thinking that way. She walked from the window and kissed her daughter again. "Hey, I love your snowman, but I've got to go. The nurse is going to be angry at me, because I'm supposed to be in bed. See you in the morning."

Meghan, always sensitive to other people's moods, asked softly, "Are you scared, Mommy?"

"A little," Claire admitted. "Are you?"

"No, I have Soldier." The child hugged her teddy bear tightly. "Daddy says I can take him to surgery with me. Would you like the teddy bear Grandma Brade gave me to take to surgery with you? I don't mind sharing."

Claire glanced at the bright new stuffed animal sitting on the bed and almost cried. "I'd like that. Will you miss him, though?"

"Not if he's with you."

She picked up the stuffed animal and held it in her arms. It would be a bond between them. "Thanks. I'll make sure he's not lonely."

Meghan smiled. "Good."

Jack had turned his back on the two of them, having problems containing his emotions. He stood, ramrod straight, staring out at the hallway. The two people he loved most in this world were going to surgery in the morning, and he didn't know if he was going to get through it without breaking down. He'd thought he was close to Meghan, but watching her with Claire he realized that the mother-child bond was stronger than any other love in the world, except that of a man for a woman. Except for his love for this woman.

After Claire turned away, Jack went to Meghan's bedside and kissed his daughter. "Get a good night's sleep."

"I will, Daddy."

"I love you, pumpkin."

Claire waited for Jack. She didn't want to cry; although the room was darkened, Meghan might hear. It would upset the child, who had already sensed Claire's despondency. Claire clutched the teddy bear to her chest and buried her face in the soft fur. Just when she thought she couldn't take another moment without bursting into tears, Jack came to take her arm, propelling her out the door.

"Good night," he called again to Meghan.

Claire managed to wave cheerily. When they got into the hallway she turned away, biting her lip to keep from sobbing out loud. The floor was quiet, few people wandered in the halls.

"I wish I could guarantee that it will be all right, Claire," Jack said quietly.

They were walking toward the elevator. She nodded as they got on, trying not to sniffle. "I know."

"The nurse will give you a sleeping pill," he went on when they got off the elevator at her floor. "I know you don't want to take anything, and normally I don't recommend them, but it will help you rest. You need to get some sleep."

She wasn't up to arguing. Besides, she knew as well as he did that she would never sleep tonight without help. "I'll take it."

He wanted to say more, and lingered when they reached the door to her room. If only they weren't so estranged. If she weren't so distant, he would take her in his arms and comfort her, kiss her, love her.

Claire was feeling restless, too. "Jack, is something wrong?"

At last he moved away, running his hand through his hair wearily. "No, everything's fine. I'll be in my office if you need me."

She wasn't fooled. "Maybe you ought to take a sleeping pill, too."

His smile, always so gentle, softened his face and saddened his eyes. "I'm the doctor, remember? Only patients get pills."

"Thank you for building a snowman with Meghan."

"It was my pleasure. I didn't mean to exclude you. You were tied up."

"I know."

"Well—" There didn't seem to be much more to say. "Good night."

"Good night, Jack."

"See you tomorrow." He'd wanted to add *I love you, Claire* but he turned away and headed toward his office. He wanted to look back, to *go* back and make things right between them. But he didn't dare. Once in his unit, he paused in Meghan's doorway and then went to the nurses' desk.

"Good evening, Jack," Nancy Ferguson said. She was alone at the nurses' desk. "Did you have dinner?"

He glanced at the redhaired nurse, hardly seeing her. All he could think of was Meghan and Claire and what might happen in the morning. "Yes, I ate earlier."

"Want some company? I was just leaving. We could go for coffee."

He shook his head. "Thanks, but if you don't mind, I think I'll pass."

Still distracted, thinking of details he might have forgotten, he started toward his office. Nancy stepped closer and placed her hand on his arm. "Jack, I need to talk to you."

"About what?" He frowned. "Nancy, is something wrong with one of the patients?"

"No," she answered, drawing a deep breath. "It's not the patients. It's us. Or rather, me," she corrected. "I'm sorry, Jack. I know this is a tough time for you, but I believe I have a right to know what's going on. Ever since your wife has come back you've closed me out of your life."

He could hardly deny her charge. Since Claire had returned, the only time he'd seen Nancy was in the unit. He knew he'd been ignoring her, and he knew he wasn't being fair to her, particularly since he also knew she was in love with him. He'd been up-front with her from the beginning, though, and surely she realized that even if he wasn't still in love with Claire, his child had to take center stage. "Nancy, I'm tired at the moment. Can we discuss this another time?"

"I guess that's what I'm trying to say, Jack. I don't see that there's anything to discuss. It seems useless to me. You'll always be in love with her."

"I'm sorry, Nancy. I wish things could be different."

"So do I." She took a deep breath. "But I can't say I'm surprised. That's what I thought. I remember you told me that the first night we went out. It was silly, but I thought maybe I could change your mind. I thought maybe I could make you love me."

Jack touched her cheek gently. "You're a great nurse, Nancy."

Although she laughed, he could tell she was close to tears. "Thanks. Just what I want to be known as—'a great nurse.'"

"Nancy—"

"Never mind," she cut in. "Don't apologize. I knew it from the beginning. I hope she doesn't hurt you, Jack. Good luck with the operation." She leaned up and kissed his cheek. "Goodbye. I'm going to ask for a transfer to another floor. I think it's best, considering everything. I can't be here and watch you with her."

"Nancy, please—"

"Don't try to make it easier, Jack," she said softly. "You'll only make it harder. I'm not telling you all this to make you feel guilty. I'm only telling you so you don't think I've abandoned you or the unit. Just remember, if you need me, I'll be around."

Odd, Jack had said those very words to Claire just a few nights ago. He watched Nancy walk away, her head held high, her shoulders shaking. She was crying, which was what he wanted to do. Why was it that love was so fickle?

The floor nurse swished by. She glanced at him with a puzzled expression. "Dr. Brady, are you all right?"

"Yes." He made a conscious effort to pull himself together. "Anything going on?"

"Nothing at the moment. Strange, huh?"

"Very," Jack agreed. Everything was so quiet, so oddly peaceful. The one night he needed something to take his mind off his problems was going to be the one night he had nothing to do. "I'll be in my office."

Once there, he flicked on the light. It illuminated the small room brightly, chasing shadows that hovered like cobwebs in his mind—shadows of disaster. He sat at his desk and opened a chart, one of the endless stacks of paperwork he could never quite keep up with. Then he picked up the model of the human kidney he kept there, the one Claire had studied so intently just a little more than a week ago, and turned it over in his hands. How inadequate his skill and education seemed at this moment. For all his knowledge, he could lose both of them in the morning, and this time it wouldn't be to a warmer climate. This time it could be for forever.

Placing the model back on the desk, he closed the chart and turned off the light. Moonlight bounced off the bright snow and streamed through the window as he flopped on the sofa and covered his eyes with one arm. Hope. They'd talked about it. He was going to need a hell of a lot of it in the morning. Along with some rest now.

Only he doubted that he would get any.

Surprisingly, Claire slept soundly. Sybil came by and they talked and joked for a while. Then the nurse gave Claire a sleeping pill that put her right out. The last thing she remembered was cuddling up to the teddy bear and yawning tiredly.

Jack breezed into the room the next morning just before she was taken to the operating room. She was ready to go. She was stripped bare of everything except pretense, and if that had been removable they'd have taken it, too, along with her panties, bobby pins, nail polish and any loose teeth she might have had in her mouth. She'd wanted to see Meghan one last time, but Jack didn't feel that was wise. Promising her they would be able to wave to each other, he walked beside the cart as the attendant wheeled her to surgery.

"Did Meghan sleep well?" Claire asked.

"Yes."

Unfortunately *he* looked like the wrath of God. He'd showered and shaved, but his eyes were red-rimmed and tired. "But you didn't," she stated. "Did you have an emergency?"

"No." He smiled, purposely. "I think I'm getting too old for the sofa. Or else too tall."

"You should buy the kind that makes into a bed."

"I'll remember that," he answered. "Maybe I'll ask for one in my quarterly report."

There was too much to be accomplished for them to talk anymore. She did get to wave to Meghan, who clutched the teddy bear in her arms and smiled, and then

Claire was whisked into a cold, bright room. Jack stayed with her until a green-clad doctor slipped a needle into her arm. "Ready to go to sleep?" the man asked.

"I just woke up. Jack—" She had a moment's panic.

"I'm here, Claire." He squeezed her hand. "I'll be here."

For the first time since she'd returned, she squeezed back. "Thank you, Jack."

She drifted off to sleep feeling the warmth of his touch. Several hours later that same warmth was the first thing she felt when she woke up. But although Jack held her hand, she felt awful. Every muscle in her body ached and her side seared with fire. Her mouth felt like dry cotton. Her vision was blurred, but she could make out his face, hovering over her. She could hear all sorts of sounds: monitors, voices, alarms, footsteps. She knew doctors and nurses were around, and that she was in the hospital recovery room, but she couldn't command her mind to think. Everything wove in and out of her consciousness like elusive ghosts.

She felt as if she were slipping away. "Jack?" she said groggily.

"I'm here, Claire."

"Is Meghan—"

"She's fine. They're operating on her now." His voice faded far away, like the room. Then it came back. Claire tried to open her eyes, but she couldn't. "Take good care of her," she heard him say to someone. "Call me if you need me. I'll be with Meghan."

The next time Claire opened her eyes a nurse stood over her. "Jack?"

"Take a deep breath and cough, Mrs. Brady," the woman said. "We need to get your lungs working well again."

Claire gave a halfhearted attempt at breathing. "I hurt."

"I know you do. It'll get better."

Why were nurses always cheerful? But Claire didn't have the energy to dwell upon it. She closed her eyes and slept.

She wasn't certain what time it was when she woke up again. She was still in the recovery room. The nurse was talking about taking her back to her room. Although she still hurt, things weren't so fuzzy now. She could feel the incision, the tight dressing on her side where they had removed her kidney, the needle where the intravenous solution dripped into her arm.

"Where's Jack?" Her throat hurt like the dickens and her mouth was still pasty. "How's Meghan?"

"Everything's fine." A new nurse, all clad in that sickening green color, said, "Just relax. Dr. Brady's tied up. He'll come to see you as soon as possible."

That was the same thing the next nurse told her—and the next and the one after that. In fact, for several hours Claire felt as though she were hearing a recording. Once back in her room she tried to stay awake, but she drifted in and out. She heard noises and confusion. Nurses woke her, made her cough, move her legs, drink some water. She glanced at the window once, thinking of the snowman and saw an occasional snowflake falling from the late-afternoon sky.

When the next nurse came in, Claire asked, "Is it going to snow?" For some crazy reason she needed to know.

"Are you awake?" the woman returned, not answering her question.

"Yes."

"Good. Take a deep breath." More cheerful orders.

"Is it going to snow?" Claire asked again, desperate to know. It was like a symbol.

"Not that I know of."

"Where's Jack?"

"Dr. Brady? They were paging him a few minutes ago. He's around, Mrs. Brady. He said he'd be here as soon as possible. I've got a shot for the pain. Turn over now."

"I want to stay awake."

"We need you to cough, and you won't cough if you're in pain. Dr. Brady's mother was here to see you a little while ago, but you were sleeping."

Claire licked her lips, trying to think. "Do you know where she is?"

"With your daughter, I believe."

"Is Meghan all right?"

"I don't know, Mrs. Brady. She's on another floor. I understand Dr. Brady's coming as soon as he can get away. Turn over now."

"Will you hand me the teddy bear?" Someone had tossed the stuffed animal in the big easy chair across the room, as if it didn't matter. As if it weren't important.

"Sure. On my way out."

But the nurse forgot, swishing out the door on sound-less shoes. Claire called, but her throat was so sore she could hardly hear herself speak. Realizing that if she wanted the teddy bear she was going to have to get it herself, she struggled to a sitting position, clutching the rails as she moved. She was dizzy and she sat for a moment on the edge of the bed. Everything was fine, she told herself. Jack was held up, that was all. He was probably seeing patients. Look how he worked, day in and day out. He was always being delayed.

Taking a deep breath, Claire stood up and locked her knees in place beneath her. Holding on to her IV stand

and whatever else she could find for support along the way, she slowly and awkwardly made her way to the chair to get the stuffed animal. Although the pain was excruciating as she bent over and picked up the toy, the tears that sprang to her eyes were from sadness. He'd promised to come and he wasn't here. Deep down inside she knew something had gone wrong. She'd felt the same way when she'd walked into his office and looked at his face.

It was dark out now. Lights had gathered on the horizon, darkening the already dark sky. She leaned her head against the windowpane. Oh, God, why wasn't he here?

"Claire, what in the world are you doing out of bed?" She wasn't certain how long she had been standing when Jack came in the door. He rushed to her side, grasping her around the waist to support her. "You've just had surgery. Get back to bed. You shouldn't be up."

"Oh, Jack, thank goodness you're here." She was so relieved to see him. "Is Meghan all right?"

She had turned to him, hoping to see joy on his features. Instead, his momentary pause was all the answer she needed. But he tried to cover up. "Let's get you back to bed," he said. "And then we'll talk."

She wasn't all right! "Jack, tell me—"

"Meghan's fine, Claire," he said. "She came through surgery fine."

"But something's wrong."

He nodded, but she knew he didn't want to admit it. "Yes, something's wrong."

"The kidney?"

"The kidney isn't working," he announced at last. "It failed."

She closed her eyes in denial. When she opened them he would tell her something different. She had to believe the operation was a success. "Jack?"

"I'm sorry, Claire."

It had all been for nothing. She couldn't even give her child a chance at life.

"Claire, there was nothing you could have done," he said softly, his tone as agonized as she felt. "Claire, look at me."

She opened her eyes.

"You tried. You gave her your kidney, but sometimes these things happen. Something was wrong with the perfusion pump. It happens occasionally, but it's something we can't predict. Sometimes we lose a kidney."

"Oh, God," Claire moaned. Although the pain was unbearable, it was in her heart and not in her side. Why Meghan's kidney? Why the one kidney she could give her child? It was incomprehensible to her to think that after everything that had happened, it had come down to a hitch in the equipment. She clutched at the back of the chair. "She's—she's so sick, Jack, I wanted—"

"I know. I wanted the same thing."

"How long—" She tried to grip her emotions the way she gripped the leather, but she was losing the battle. "How long will she last?"

"We'll get her back on dialysis, Claire. We'll keep her as healthy as we can."

She noticed he'd evaded her question. "But she's so sick. She builds up toxins fast."

"Yes," he admitted.

"Is your mother with her?"

"Yes, she's staying the night if that's all right with you."

"I'm glad. If I can't be with her, at least she has someone."

"Claire, you can't blame yourself."

She couldn't stand to look at him. She was going to fall apart. Any moment now she was going to start screaming hysterically. She glanced out the window again. Huge snowflakes swirled in the air and a cold, bitter wind kicked up the snow from the ground. It seemed somehow fitting that it was going to storm, after all.

Jack came up behind her, taking her by the arm. "You're going to fall down, Claire. You're still weak. You shouldn't be out of bed. Let me help you."

"I wanted the teddy bear." She smiled sadly, clinging to the pert little animal.

"You should have asked for it."

"I did, but the nurse didn't listen. I had to get it. I'm fine."

"No, you're not." Although she resisted momentarily, he held her tightly, enfolding her against his body and tucking her head below his chin. "Don't fight it, Claire." He stroked her hair gently. "Cry. Go ahead and let it out."

She couldn't hold back any longer. The gentleness of his touch, the emotion of the moment, caused tears to start down her face. Huge sobs racked her body. "Jack—"

"Come on. Let me hold you."

He scooped her up in his arms and held her cradled against his chest. Hooking his foot around the easy chair, he moved it beside the bed. But instead of lying her down in bed, he sat in the chair and huddled her in his lap while she clung to him and cried.

All the tears weren't hers. "It's going to be all right, Claire," he said raggedly, brushing his lips lightly over her forehead. "We'll make it through this."

"I'm sorry, Jack."

"Don't be."

"For everything. I'm sorry for everything. God, how I love her." Claire snuggled closer to him, needing his strength. Oddly, even though she'd had surgery, she wasn't uncomfortable. She felt protected in his arms. Comforted.

Jack's throat tightened even more and he kept brushing his hand across her hair, soothing her. "So do I."

They sat for a long time with him holding her. The narcotic was starting to take effect and after a while Claire grew sleepy. A nurse came by, pausing in the doorway. "Is Mrs. Brady all right, Dr. Brady?"

"She's fine." Claire could hear his chest rumble, but the words blurred as she drifted deeper into sleep.

"Do you need anything?"

"Yes, please. Call upstairs and tell them to get Meghan on the list for a kidney. They'll need to phone in the information to the bureau tonight, and we need to restart dialysis right away."

"Anything else?"

He nodded decisively. "Yes. Tell Dr. Davies to take my calls tonight. Leave word not to disturb me unless it's about Meghan. I'm going to stay here with Mrs. Brady."

"All right. Let me know if she needs anything."

"Don't worry, I'll take care of her." When the nurse left he reached for a blanket and tucked it around the woman in his arms. Then he brushed his lips across her forehead before he leaned back in the chair and closed his eyes. "I love you, Claire," he murmured softly. "God, how I love you."

Chapter 7

Claire recovered quickly. Within two days she was up on her feet, pacing the halls and looking for something to do. In little more than a week she was begging to be released. Meghan had been put back on dialysis and although they managed to visit frequently, Claire was anxious to go home or, rather, to Care House. She could see her daughter at any time then.

Jack wasn't at all pleased by her requests for an early discharge. Ever since the operation, he had hovered over her like a mother hen. "Look," he said, watching her pull a brush through her hair as she got ready to leave. Only moments before, Hal Davies had signed the papers authorizing her to go. She had finished dressing in a pair of loose slacks and blouse when Jack had hurried into the room, his white coat billowing behind him as usual. "Just because they've taken out your stitches doesn't mean you can run around doing whatever you please. You had major surgery. In order to get to your kidney we had to go through a major muscle group, and you aren't totally healed yet. It'll be six weeks before you've fully recuperated. In the meantime you can't lift—"

"What am I going to lift at Care House?" Claire cut in, smiling at him in amusement. He was so concerned. His forehead was all puckered up in a frown.

"What about here, visiting Meghan?"

"I'll lift her dinner tray."

"Too heavy."

"All right," Claire answered, placing the brush down and letting her hair swing free around her shoulders. She slipped her shoes on and tossed her sweater over her shoulders. "I won't lift her dinner tray. I won't lift a single thing. Jack, please, I'm fine. I feel fine. I look fine. I act fine. I'm going to *be* fine."

His scowl didn't go away. "I still think you should let your mother come and help you."

"Come and help me do what? My mother would only complicate matters. Think about it. Where would she stay? Rooms are at a premium at Care House."

He paced the floor, obviously unappeased. At last he stopped and said abruptly, "If you won't accept your mother's help, then why won't you go to my mother's? Just for a week or two until you're back on your feet."

Claire had to laugh. She had reached an agreement of sorts with his mother, but they hadn't come *that* far. "Oh, sure, and argue with her all day long. Jack, we're trying our best to be friends."

"I don't like you being alone," he said.

"I won't be alone." She gestured around. "You always seem to forget, this is a hospital." And he was here. But she didn't add that. Since that night when he'd held her, she'd grown more dependent on him for emotional support. For the most part their relationship was easy, pleasant, mutually understanding. Occasionally she could see flashes of need, of longing, in his expression, but he would turn away and they didn't discuss it. It felt as if she'd seen more of him in the past week than she had in the entire year they'd been married, and she certainly knew a lot more about him.

"That's exactly my point, Claire. You're being discharged from the hospital."

"I'm only going across the street. Believe me, Jack, I'll be fine. How much trouble can I have when the highlight of my day will be coming back and forth to see Meghan? I don't even have to go outside. Don't you think you're being a bit ridiculous?"

He sighed. "All right, Claire. You're right, I'm sorry. I'm overreacting. I'm worried, though. Just use your common sense. Okay?"

She nodded. Dr. Davies had already given her her postoperative instructions. No drinking, no driving, no major decisions. Of course, she'd already made lots of major decisions just by putting Meghan on dialysis. No lifting or tugging. She needed lots of rest and a good, well-balanced diet.

"Do you have an appointment to see Hal?"

Claire was still taking special vitamins and she had to have her blood drawn frequently to keep on top of the blood dyscrasia. "Yes, I'm seeing him next week."

"I guess that's it, then." Jack picked up the bag of junk she'd accumulated. It was beyond her why she was taking her thermometer and wash basin, but the nurse had packed them in a huge plastic bag, along with her nightgown and robe. "Ready? I'll walk you over."

She glanced at her watch. "Aren't you due in surgery?"

"I rearranged my schedule. I have a few hours off. I wanted to be sure to get you settled in."

"Jack, please."

"Please what?"

Claire shook her head in dismay when he glanced at her with a true question in his eyes. "Never mind."

Although he was still being overprotective, she wasn't about to argue with him. She'd let him walk her across the street and hang up her clothes. Then she'd walk back with him and visit her daughter.

But when they got to Care House Jack mentioned that Meghan had just returned from dialysis.

"When did they finish?"

"About two o'clock," he said.

Claire glanced back at her watch, knowing Meghan would probably sleep for several hours. "Well, then, I guess there isn't much to do."

"You could rest."

"I'm not tired."

Since the room was darkened, she went to open the drapes to let in the sunshine. All week the weather had been cold and blustery. Now it was gently snowing. Huge, fat snowflakes fell lazily from the sky. She could see the snowman Meghan had built at the side of the building. Although she'd looked at it every day, from this view it seemed even more like a giant white apparition sticking up out of the ground. The snowman's side was still flat and it still needed a smile.

Jack moved to stand alongside her. Noticing the snowman, he grinned. "It really is kind of pathetic looking, isn't it?"

"Yes." She glanced at him. "Jack, let's fix it."

"What?" He frowned at her as though he thought she'd lost her mind.

"Let's fix it." Without waiting for his answer she rushed to the closet and grabbed the jacket, scarf and mittens he had given her and headed toward the door.

"Where are you going?"

"To fix the snowman. It needs a smile."

"You've just had an operation. You can't go out there."

"Why not? I told you I feel fine." As she spoke, Claire pulled on the coat and tossed the scarf around her neck. She pulled her hair out of the collar as she hurried down the hall toward the elevators.

Jack started after her. "You could hurt yourself."

"I won't. I'll be all right."

"Claire, this is stupid."

For once she didn't disagree. She couldn't say what force was propelling her out into the cold, cold day, but for some reason she felt compelled to fix the snowman. On the one hand she could recognize that her reasoning was all mixed up with guilt, with not being able to build it with Meghan, or with the failure of the kidney, *her* kidney. On the other hand, she knew it was something she had to do. She shot him a glance over her shoulder. "Do you have a coat?"

"Claire—"

She kept walking, heading down the steps instead of waiting for the elevator. "Don't harp at me, Jack. If you want to do anything, help me. I'm going to fix the snowman if it's the last thing I do."

He shook his head. "This is crazy, Claire."

Claire opened the door to the ground floor.

"Wait a minute." Before they went outside Jack paused to borrow a jacket from an elderly man who sat at the front desk handing out visitor passes. "I'll bring it right back," he promised. Then, without skipping a beat, he said to Claire, "I don't understand. You hate the cold. You hate snow."

"This has nothing to do with snow."

"I never realized you could be so stubborn, Claire."

"There are a lot of things you don't know about me, Jack."

"You're impetuous."

"You're overbearing."

"And you don't listen," he returned angrily. "Dammit, Claire, I'm a doctor, and I'm telling you this is dangerous."

"And I'm telling you I'm doing it," she answered. "Besides, I'm not a patient anymore; and even if I were, you're not my doctor. Hal is." Once out the door, Claire, more determined than ever, tromped across the frozen ground to the snowman. It was chilly outside and she shivered as the cold wind ruffled her hair, but she scooped up snow in her hand and started packing it around the bottom, filling out the flat part that had bothered her.

Jack gave a disgusted sound, standing over her. "Claire, can I try one more time to talk you out of this?"

She didn't bother to look at him. "No."

"Fine." He knelt down. Without further comment, he scooped up some snow. "I'll build," he said quietly. "You sculpt. And tuck your scarf tighter around your neck. I don't want you to get sick."

Claire paused. She hated arguing with him. This past week they'd gotten along so well. "Were you this protective of Meghan when you two built the snowman?"

"Yes," he answered gruffly.

"No wonder it's so funny looking. I've never built a snowman before, but I imagine it takes time and patience."

He smiled at her. "If you hadn't just had surgery, Claire Brady, I'd rub this snow in your face."

"My, you're vindictive."

He laughed. "Let's get to work so we can get back inside."

Actually, Jack did most of the work. Claire hadn't realized how quickly she would tire, yet she patted each scoop of snow until the bottom of the snowman bulged into a beautiful, round shape. Several people paused to watch the two of them struggle in the snow, but after a few moments in the cold, went on into the hospital, shivering and shaking their heads.

At last Claire was satisfied with the shape. She stood up and frowned. "He still needs a smile."

Jack shrugged. "I don't have any coal. Pennies will have to do. You know, Meghan was much more cooperative," he remarked as he reached into his pocket, pulled out several coins, and placed them on the snowman, making a merry face.

"She's a child. That's perfect." As a final touch, Claire took off her scarf and placed it around the fat white neck. She stood back to admire their handiwork. "There. Isn't he great?"

"It is an improvement," Jack agreed, standing beside her. He glanced down at her. "You really shouldn't leave your scarf."

"I want him to have it." Surprisingly she wasn't at all chilled. Her cheeks were ruddy; she could feel them tingle. But she felt invigorated, though a bit tired. When a huge snowflake fluttered past her nose, she stuck out her tougue to catch it.

Jack seemed amused. "What was that all about?"

Claire laughed. "Meghan told me she caught a snowflake on her tongue. I thought I'd try it. It tickles."

"No wonder," he told her. "They're polluted."

"Snowflakes?"

"Haven't you ever heard of acid rain? Moisture comes down through the atmosphere and picks up pollutants."

Claire glanced at the pretty crystals swirling through the air. It seemed a sacrilege. "That's awful."

"Sad but true. I always thought of snowflakes as being nature's way of making rain pretty."

She glanced back at him, surprised. "What a lovely way to think of it."

"I'm poetic."

She studied him a long moment. "You are poetic, you know."

"I'm also cold, Claire."

She shrugged to indicate the huge down jacket she was wearing. "I'm toasty warm. By the way, when nature makes a blizzard, what's she doing?"

He grinned. "Getting back at people who think they can live here."

"I thought you liked Minnesota."

"I do," he answered. "I just don't like standing out in ten-below-zero weather in a coat that's too small for me."

"Jack, where do you live?"

He frowned at her again, puzzled by her odd question. "In a condo a couple miles from here. Why?"

"I just wondered. What's it like?"

He paused thoughtfully. "I'm there so seldom I really don't know how to describe it," he said finally.

"Could we go see it?" It would be good to get away from the hospital. This was the first time she'd been out of the building in weeks, and even though the weather was crisp, she was enjoying herself.

"Now?"

"Do you still have some time off?"

He checked his watch. "Yes. Several hours."

"What else are you going to do?"

"Paperwork." He smiled again, then grabbed her elbow. "Come on, let's go." But he hesitated again when they got to the sidewalk.

"Is something wrong?" she asked.

"Just that I don't know whether you should walk to the car or if I should go get it and come back for you."

"Where's it parked?"

"In the lot."

"I'll walk to the car. I'm sure I can make it a block or two. But why don't we stop to get your coat? You look so cold that I'm beginning to feel sorry for you."

"That's a first."

They tried to hurry, but once they arrived back at the hospital it took forty-five minutes to get out. He was off duty, but people still asked him questions, sought his advice. As usual, Jack took it all in stride. Surprisingly it didn't bother Claire much. She stood beside him, listening, nodding to people she'd met, waiting until they could get away.

"How long has it been since you've used your car?" she asked when they got to the parking lot and he headed toward a compact sedan that looked more like an igloo than an automobile. Snow at least a foot deep was mounded over the hood and roof.

"About a week." He brushed at the snow, trying to find the door. "If I disappear, send a Saint Bernard. Better yet, just give me the brandy."

Claire smiled at his joke. It took him several minutes to clear off the car, and when he was done they climbed inside. After a quick drive they reached his condominium. His place was located in a renovated area near downtown Minneapolis, close to the hospital. Jack pulled into a private parking space and helped her out her side. "I have a housekeeper who comes in a couple of times a week, so the place should be clean. You might brace yourself, though. I am a bachelor."

His apartment was sparse, starkly modern, and very striking as well as spotlessly clean. When they walked inside, Claire stood to stare at the clean lines and shiny surfaces. It looked like something out of a magazine. The decor was mostly Oriental. Black-lacquered furniture was set in small alcoves behind bamboo screens. The only table decorations were jade vases and intricately carved ivory sculptures. Floor-to-ceiling mirrors adorned the walls, and windows stretched across the entire front, showcasing the city and giving a sense of openness. Carrying out the Oriental theme, the white carpet contrasted with the black silk sofa and chairs.

"It's gorgeous," Claire murmured, glancing around. The feeling of spaciousness was enhanced by the adjoining open kitchen, which even from where she stood she could see was all stainless steel and stark-white appliances. "Who's your decorator?"

"Me. I kind of used our apartment as a guide, and I guess I got so accustomed to not having much, that when I could have things, I didn't know what to get, and so I have very little."

They'd decorated sparsely when they'd been married, but it hadn't been like this. And what furniture he did have was what made it so dramatic. She traced her finger across a highly polished table as he took their jackets and tossed them on a nearby chair. "It's stunning, Jack."

"Do you like it?"

"Yes. Absolutely."

He studied her thoughtfully. "What would you have done differently?"

She looked around, considering. "Nothing."

"Sometimes it seems so cold to me. It's not a family place."

Claire frowned her disagreement. "I'm not sure about that. Kids do get things dirty, but furnishings aren't what make a home homey. I think it's more the love inside."

"That's a nice thought," he said. "I guess the place is such a contrast to me, sometimes. My office is so cluttered."

She turned back to him. "That's because you live there. And you don't have a housekeeper come in."

"True," he agreed.

She glanced at the television. The screen took up the entire back half of the room. "Is that for *Frankenstein Meets Wolfman*?"

"Yes, the fangs show up better. Want something to drink? I could make some tea."

"Sounds good." Claire followed him into the kitchen, wandering behind him, still marveling at the furnishings. Several hand-embroidered Japanese prints adorned one wall.

"You ought to sit down." Jack motioned to a chair. "You've been on your feet a long time."

"I'm fine, Jack," she told him for what seemed the hundredth time. "All right," she gave in, sitting down on a high stool when he narrowed his eyes and glared at her. She *was* tired. "I'll rest."

"Want some supper?"

"You have food here?" Since he'd admitted to coming here so seldom, she had imagined the refrigerator was barren.

"Not really, but we could order in. Do you mind?"

"No." She was surprised. It wasn't very often that he relinquished his duties. "Who's covering for you, anyway?"

"Hal. You know, I was thinking of asking him to be my partner," Jack went on as he filled a teakettle with water and put it on the stove. "I'd like to get someone to help me in the unit, and with all my patients."

With every word she grew increasingly surprised. Jack *sharing* a practice? It seemed as much a sacrilege as the snowflakes being polluted. "Dr. Davies seems a very good physician," she remarked.

Jack nodded. "He is. And we get along well." He glanced at her. "What do you think?"

"About Hal?"

"About ordering something in."

"Sounds great."

"Pizza?"

The man never ceased to amaze her. "You have a good memory Jack."

He picked up the phone and started dialing. "With you it's easy, Claire. I think you married me because you thought I could cook Italian food."

She laughed. Not only could he not cook Italian, the first few months he hadn't even been able to boil water. Of course, neither could she, and in fact she still wasn't very good at it. "We were really something, weren't we?"

"Yes," he said quietly. "We were."

How quickly the subject changed. They were talking about the happy past again. She looked at him and her heart began to thud. This wasn't the time to let him get to her. She was vulnerable because of her surgery and Meghan's illness. She slipped off the stool and wandered back into the living room. "Where did you get all the Japanese prints?"

"The art shop." Jack came up behind her, handing her a cup of tea. "Be careful, it's hot. Sugar's in it. Two spoons, right?"

"Yes." He sat on the sofa and Claire took a seat opposite him.

"The pizza and soda will be here in a few minutes." He took a sip of tea. "So. Tell me, what have you been doing the past four years?"

What an odd question. It was as if she'd just arrived in town ten minutes ago. "Work. What have you done?"

He laughed. "Touché." Then he sighed. "Sometimes I have trouble talking to you, Claire. I don't know what to say."

Before they hadn't had to talk. Their communication had been silent. "I know," she answered. "But a lot of time has passed, hasn't it?"

"Yes."

"I got a job as a secretary," she went on, for some reason really wanting to talk with him. "I worked for an accounting firm."

He leaned forward. "Claire, I wish you would have let me send you alimony."

"I didn't want alimony, Jack."

"You wanted to be rid of me."

"I needed to break my ties. I really didn't want to hurt you."

They'd reached a new level of understanding lately. Now he nodded, for the first time truly realizing what she'd been up against, how difficult their life together had been for her and how tough it had been for her to pick up and leave. "Do you ever regret not going back to school?"

"I went to secretarial school."

"No, I mean college."

That was something she'd thought about a lot herself. "No. Strange as it seems, I'm not the career type. I'm perfectly content being a mother."

"You're good at it."

"Thank you." She hesitated, questioning the wisdom of continuing the subject, but plunging on anyway. "And you're a good father, Jack."

"I'm learning."

"You're a good doctor, too."

"Do you think so?" He seemed touched by her compliment and at the same time surprised.

"Oh, yes, very good. Don't you know that?"

"I like to think it."

They had just finished their tea when pizza came. Jack paid for it and carried it into the living room, moving some things from the coffee table to place it down. "I'll get some plates and napkins."

"Are you sure you want to eat in here?"

"Why not?"

"Everything's so nice."

"So let's mess it up. The place needs to look lived-in once in a while."

It seemed silly to keep sitting in the chair. Claire moved to the sofa where they could both eat. "Do you still like the mushy center pieces?" she called, unable to resist sneaking a corner and eating it. The smell was absolutely marvelous. For the past week all she'd had was hospital food, which had started tasting suspiciously like cardboard.

"They're the best. Don't tell me you've changed," he answered, coming back into the room and handing her a glass of soda and a wad of napkins.

"Oh, no, I still like the ends. But if you don't hurry, I might eat it all."

He sat beside her. "You always did have a healthy appetite."

"I was a pig," she admitted.

The pizza tasted heavenly. Claire ate until she couldn't take another bite. She tossed down her napkin, stuffed and contented. "Mmm, that was good."

Jack was full, too. He pushed away the mess and leaned his head on the back of the sofa. "Great," he agreed and yawned. "Now I could take a nice, long nap. Too bad I don't have about ten hours off."

She glanced at him with an expression of admonition. "I can see it now. When you get old you're going to get fat, Jack. You'll be the type who'll do nothing but eat and sleep."

"Look who's talking," he countered, lifting his head up to peer at her. "I was counting those pieces, Claire Brady, and you packed in quite a few calories."

"Must I remind you I've been existing on hospital food for the past several weeks?"

"Point taken." He lifted his feet up onto the coffee table and crossed them contentedly. Afternoon had turned to night. Although it was February the days were short in the Midwest. Bright lights started flickering on all over the city, signaling the darkness. "You know, I think that's the first uninterrupted meal I've had in the past several years."

"You should take more time off, Jack."

He nodded. "It's been nice."

Being with him, sharing the moments, had been nice.

"Do you want more children, Claire?"

She frowned at him. "What brought that on?"

"Our previous discussion. Do you?"

She gave an offhand shrug. "I don't know. That's kind of a moot point, isn't it, considering that I'm unmarried?"

"That could change."

"It could," she agreed, nodding. But it wasn't likely. To date she hadn't met a single man that compared to him.

"I'd like more children," he went on. She glanced at him as he spoke, "I enjoyed having brothers and sisters. I love Meghan. And the kids on the unit are so special to me."

"You care too much, Jack," she said. As she had. "Too deeply."

"I know." For the longest time he stared at her, the blue of his eyes sincere, then intense. When had their mood changed? They'd gone from friendly camaraderie to smoldering mutual awareness in just a few brief moments. All of a sudden she looked at him and the friendship was gone. In its place was dark, raw passion. This was a man beside her—a virile man with wants and needs and desires.

"Jack?"

Since they were sitting so close together it seemed natural for him to lean toward her. It also seemed natural for him to kiss her. Gently he cupped his hand along her cheek and lowered his mouth to hers. Claire didn't resist. Even if she'd had the strength, she didn't have the inclination. She wanted this. No matter what agonies she'd suffered before, what hurts, for some crazy reason she wanted his touch, his embrace, his love. Ever since that night when he'd held her, she'd felt close to him, as if she belonged in his arms being loved by him, loving him.

The kiss was everything she had thought it would be: soft and poignant, yet at the same time hard and passionate. Jack's lips moved over hers commandingly, seeking and demanding. Wanting. A fiery blaze started to flicker at her belly and she moaned, slipping her arms around his neck.

Jack must have thought she was hurt. He drew away quickly, as though just realizing he was kissing her, holding her. "I'm sorry, Claire," he said hoarsely, raking a hand through his hair. "With all my protestations of concern, I forgot you just had surgery."

"You weren't hurting me."

"But I could have. Good Lord, I'm a doctor." With a heavy sigh, he got up and paced to the window, standing there looking out and rubbing the back of his neck in frustration.

"You're also a man, Jack," she said quietly.

At last he turned back to look at her. "A mere mortal? Yes, I'm afraid so," he continued. "You must be tired by now. I'll take you back."

Claire *was* tired, and her fatigue almost matched her confusion. "Jack, I'm sorry."

"For what?"

"Us." She got up, too, and went to stand beside him at the window, wanting to explain. Tiny lights shimmered from all over town. Since they hadn't turned on any lamps, his face was in shadow, except for the city lights. "For the way it ended."

"Now or then?"

"Both."

Gently he swept her hair back from her face. The gesture had become so familiar over the past few weeks, like his touch, his caring. There in the dark they were two souls alone in the world, needing each other. "It's odd how things change, isn't it?" he murmured softly. "And then again they don't change at all. A couple of weeks ago I asked you out to dinner to discuss our differences and we didn't get to go, and now I don't want us to have any differences at all. I never wanted us to have any differences."

"That's not possible, Jack. People always have differences. It's only natural."

"I know. I may be overbearing, but I do eventually learn, Claire."

She laughed. "I'm not sure I can make the same claim. I just tend to be stubborn."

"Very. It's late," he said. "We should go back."

They both jumped when the telephone rang. Claire glanced toward the kitchen, her heart thudding with sudden anxiety. They'd waited too long. "Who do you think it is?"

"The hospital," Jack said with certainty.

"Meghan?"

"I doubt it." He went to answer. "She was fine when we left. I called the unit just before we went out the door. Don't worry, it's probably something else."

Claire gathered up their mess while she waited for him. She knew from what he was saying that the call wasn't about their daughter, and she breathed a sigh of relief.

A few moments later Jack came to take the garbage from her. "It was just a consultation. I have to go by Parkside Hospital after I drop you off. Meghan's fine."

"Thanks."

He smiled at her and placed his hand over hers, squeezing gently. "No. Thank *you*, Claire, for getting me away for a while. I can't tell you how pleasant it's been."

She felt pleased. "We'll have to do it again sometime."

"You're on." He held up her jacket, helping her slip it on. "Bundle up, now."

"I'm fine, Jack."

He had been standing at the door. Abruptly he turned back and went to his closet. Taking a scarf from the shelf, he placed it around her neck, tucking it tightly. "You're not really fine, Claire," he murmured. "Neither am I, but I think we're getting there. At least, I hope the wounds are starting to heal."

Chapter 8

When they got back to the hospital, Meghan was awake and playing a game with Kathleen. Every day that the child had gone for dialysis she'd gotten increasingly stronger. Despite having had surgery, her complexion had lost its pasty look and color had come back into her cheeks. If only the change would be permanent, Claire thought. But she knew it wasn't. The only halfway permanent cure was another kidney, for which they'd have to wait. And hope.

Claire didn't want to think about the possibility of another failure. Would they apply for another? And another? At what point would they get turned down?

She smiled brightly. "So, what have you girls been up to all evening?"

Kathleen was the first to answer. "We played charades with the shrink." Her parents were still away, and she was growing lonelier than ever. She rolled her eyes expressively. "Bor-ing."

"I liked it," Meghan spoke up. "It was fun."

Kathleen snorted. "That's because you were a butterfly. I got to be a turnip."

"I'm sure there's some significance to that," Jack said, laughing; but he looked as puzzled as everyone else. "Unfortunately I don't have time to figure it out. I'll talk to you all later." From the moment they'd walked back into the hospital he'd been besieged by one phone call after the other, one page after the other, and he still had to go to Parkside Hospital for the consultation he'd agreed to earlier. "Take care and get some rest. All of you." He kissed Meghan, tweaked Kathleen's toes and winked at Claire before he headed off down the hall.

"Good night, Daddy," Meghan called. Then she glanced at Claire. "I pretended to fly."

"I'll bet that was fun." Claire realized they were still talking about charades.

"Oh, it was a ball," Kathleen said. "I got smushed. Then somebody cooked me."

Claire couldn't help laughing. She wished she'd seen the episode.

"Mommy, where's Hero?"

Claire frowned at her child. "Hero?"

"The teddy bear I loaned you," Meghan explained. "The one Grandma Brady gave me. You didn't leave it in the hospital, did you?"

"Oh, no." Claire should have known. "He's in my room across the street."

"Are you taking good care of him?"

She nodded gravely. "Very good care. He sleeps with me every night, just like Soldier sleeps with you." She leaned down to kiss Meghan's cheek. "And if you don't mind, I think I'll go over and go to bed now. I'm awfully tired."

Kathleen giggled. "No wonder. I'd be tired too, if I spent the afternoon with Dr. Brady."

Although the speed at which news traveled around the hospital continued to amaze Claire, she smiled at the outspoken teenager. "I'll bet you would, particularly if you'd eaten pizza."

"That's all you did?"

"Yes."

"You know Mrs. B., you're no fun. You need to start watching TV. Give you some ideas."

Claire grinned. "You have too many ideas, Kathy." She nodded toward Meghan. "It might be wise to keep some of them under your hat."

Kathleen glanced at Meghan, too, catching on quickly. "Ahh. Gotcha."

"Good night." Claire went out of the room, shaking her head at the antics of fifteen-year-old girls. After telling the floor nurse where she would be, she went across the street to Care House. She didn't get to bed right away, because just as she was unlocking her door, Sybil came from the lounge area.

"Well, good evening," the western woman drawled. "I was wondering when you were going to get back. Here you need your rest, and you've been off gallivanting most of the day."

Claire couldn't believe it. Was there anyone who didn't know what she'd done this afternoon? "I was with Jack."

"Yes, I know. I saw you building the snowman." Sybil frowned. "Does that mean you're planning to stay here in Minnesota?"

Claire frowned back. "Why would you think that?"

Sybil shrugged. "It seemed symbolic. You were out there struggling, trying to fix the snowman. You know.

Like you were accepting the good and the bad. And you've got to admit the weather's been bad.''

Although Claire figured the gossip mill had perpetuated her obsession with the cold and snow, she didn't know what to say. She hadn't even thought about their excursion except for how it applied to Meghan. One thing was true: the weather had been bad. ''You don't seem to mind the weather here at all.''

The woman shook her head. ''This is mild compared to Montana. Sometimes in the winter we get roof-high drifts, and it can drop to forty, fifty below zero.''

''What do you do?''

''Not much you can do but accept it. Sometimes the cows starve to death and we'll be stranded for weeks at a time. No phone. Just what food you've put up.'' She shrugged again. ''But you know spring's coming eventually. Believe me, it's not half as bad as having a kid who needs a transplant. Now *that*'s helpless. Did you hear Robbie's going home?''

''You're going back to Montana?'' Claire was astonished. She'd been so wrapped up in Meghan, she hadn't kept up with Robbie. She knew he hadn't had surgery, though.

''Well, no, we're staying here for now. He's stabilized on dialysis. Since he only has to come back two or three times a week, Dr. Brady said he could be discharged until we find a kidney and he gets a transplant. Live a more normal life—school and home and all those good things.''

''All those good things'' weren't so easy to provide. ''Where are you going to stay?''

''I rented an apartment near the hospital. It's real cute. Just a couple of rooms. A nice kitchen. You'll have to come over. I'll have to go to work part-time to pay the rent, but I think it's going to be a good move." Sybil gave her a long, assessing glance. "You know, speaking of good, you look damn terrific for a woman who had surgery just a week ago."

Claire smiled. "It's the ten pounds I lost."

"I should be so lucky." Sybil shook her head. "The last time I had surgery I gained weight on the dextrose and water they gave me as intravenous. Well, I guess we have to fatten you up. Want to go for breakfast in the morning?"

"Sounds good."

"See you then. Get some rest, huh?"

It seemed everyone had the same advice. "I will."

"By the way, I love the snowman—the scarf is great."

"Thanks."

Claire unlocked her door and turned on the light. The drapes were still open and she went to the window to look outside. The red scarf she'd tied around the snowman fluttered in the breeze. In a way she supposed her struggle to fix the thing had been a sign of acceptance. There was so much she needed to accept: Meghan's illness, her love for Jack, the cold, snow and wind. If only their wounds *were* healing.

She sighed and closed the drapes.

Yes, if only...

With a shake of her head Claire turned out the lights and crawled into bed. "If only" was something she could think about tomorrow. Right now, everyone was right: she needed to get some rest.

Jack arrived before Sybil the next morning. Claire was expecting her friend, and she opened the door without thinking when he knocked. "Come on in," she said, turning around to strip off her nightgown and throw on some clothes. She'd slept through the alarm again. "I'll be ready in a moment. You always catch me undressed."

"Excuse me, Claire."

The deep, masculine voice surprised her, grating huskily along her spine. She swung around, clutching her nightgown to her body, and blushed. "Jack."

He smiled. "Good morning."

"Good morning," she answered lamely. In a way it seemed silly to be embarrassed. It wasn't as if he hadn't seen her undressed before. They'd been married. And just eight days ago he'd stood by while she'd had major surgery. She'd been stark naked then. Then afterward he'd washed her, helped her brush her teeth, walked with her as she'd taken her first steps down the hall.

But this was different. This was man to woman. She pushed her hair back nervously. "What can I do for you, Jack? Is something wrong?"

"No," he answered. "Everything's fine. I just wondered if you wanted to join me for breakfast."

"I told Sybil I'd eat with her."

"Is she still here at Care House? I thought she'd rented an apartment."

"I don't think it's ready yet," Claire said.

"Well, then—" Jack seemed undaunted "—since you have a breakfast partner, how about dinner instead?"

"Tonight?"

He smiled that slow grin that lit up his face. "You have another engagement?"

"No, I'm just uncomfortable." She gestured to her state of undress. "I don't have any clothes on."

"I see."

"In fact you do see. Plenty."

He actually laughed. "Sorry. The pun was unintended."

She didn't know what else to say. Or what to do. He didn't seem about to leave and though he'd laughed, he hadn't turned around or stopped looking at her. "Where do you want to go?"

"Tonight?"

That had been her line. "Turn around, Jack," she said, making her voice firm by willpower alone. "And let me get some clothes on."

He seemed surprised by her brusque tone. "Sorry, Claire," he replied. "I don't mean to embarrass you, but you really haven't changed at all. I can't seem to stop looking at you. You're still absolutely beautiful."

For all her bravado, she felt her breath catch in her throat. Her knees went weak, listening to his soft words. Why was it that this one particular man could throw her so with just a look, a touch? While he stood there staring at her with raw desire, there was so much more in his eyes: love and caring and gentle devotion.

"Don't, Jack. Don't make it difficult."

"It's already difficult, Claire," he answered. "At least for me. You know I still want that explanation. One of these days we have to talk."

There was no way out. "Yes. I know."

For once he wasn't polite. He stared at her—hard. "Tonight. Seven. Be ready." Then he turned and walked away.

Sybil appeared in the doorway just as he left. The Montana woman dodged deftly. "Morning."

"Morning," he answered gruffly, but he didn't stop.

Sybil watched his disappearing figure and then swung her gaze to Claire, who was standing in the middle of the room with her nightgown draped around her body. "Foul mood?"

"Very." Claire stared after him, too—or rather, at the empty spot where he'd stood—and thought for a moment. "Have you ever had surgery, Sybil?"

"Twice. Why?"

"How long is it before you can make love?"

The other woman shrugged. "That depends on what you've had done. Two, three weeks, maybe. I guess it would also depend on what you do and how you do it; whether you're into acrobatics or just lying there letting it happen. You going to make love?"

Claire went to the closet to pull out some clothes. "No, but I figure that's how long I'll be safe."

"From Dr. Brady?" Sybil arched a single eyebrow in a question. "If that's true, then I think you're looking at it wrong. I'd call that unfortunate rather than safe."

Claire smiled, amused. "Then maybe I'd better get up my strength."

"I would. Of course, being from Montana, I like my men wild."

But Claire didn't have to worry about Jack and sex. He was back in his even mood that night when he picked her up. He arrived at her door at seven o'clock exactly, dressed in slacks and a knit shirt that were quite different from his usual, more formal attire. Yet he still looked long and lean and incredibly handsome.

"Where are we going?" she asked, taking in his casual clothing. The shirt was soft and well-worn, stretching tautly across his chest.

"I thought we'd eat across the street."

"The Italian restaurant?"

"Yes, why?"

Emilio's Café was full of memories for them both. "I don't know. I guess I'm not sure that's the right place to go."

"It's great for spaghetti."

So he wasn't going to acknowledge any fears. Interesting. "We had pizza last night. Are you sure you want tomato sauce again?"

"There's an old expression: you can't eat too much Italian food or drink too much Italian wine."

"I thought it was that you can't be too rich or too thin."

He smiled. "I think you're right. Want to go somewhere else?"

"Not really." If he could chase ghosts all night long, so could she. "Let me get my coat."

The restaurant hadn't changed much from when they'd gone there four years ago. Emilio had upscaled the decor a bit, but it was still casual and very Italian, right down to the red-and-white checkered tablecloths and candle-dripped wine bottles. When Jack pushed open the door, Claire's mouth watered from the odor of freshly baked garlic bread, oregano and tomato sauce.

Steering her in front of him, he headed for a booth in the back—their booth. At least once a week they would eat here, stuffing themselves, taking the leftovers home for other meals. Emilio would laugh and serenade them—his two favorite lovers—singing Italian songs in his off-key voice.

Claire had to force the memories away. She slid into the booth and slipped off her jacket as Jack sat down across from her. Music played and people laughed. Almost before they were seated, Emilio came from the kitchen.

"Clarisa!" He threw his arms up into the air, his eyes lighting up with pleasure as he came to their table and hugged her. "My Clarisa! You are back! And as beautiful as ever."

She laughed and hugged him back. "Still the old charmer, I see, handing out the compliments."

"Ah! You wound me." He clutched at his heart. Then his expression grew serious. "The bambino, she is sick?"

Of the few the people she'd known in Minneapolis, Emilio was one of the ones who had taken an interest in Meghan when she'd been a baby—a squalling, unhappy baby. "Yes," Claire answered, "but she's not a baby anymore. She's a big girl now. All of four years old."

"I see her soon?"

Why not? Claire nodded. "Yes, I'll bring her in soon."

"I give her spaghetti. Make her big and strong." Apparently Emilio ascribed to the "you can't get too much Italian" theory, too. "She look like you?"

"No, like Jack."

"Ah, but beautiful, no?"

"Beautiful, yes." Claire smiled.

Emilio gave a sly look at Jack, but he spoke to Claire. "You stay here this time? You no go California?"

"I'm not sure what I'm going to do," she answered honestly. Although she was conscious of Jack's presence, she didn't try to hedge. "A lot's going to depend on Meghan."

"She be fine. You will see. You eat now. Forget sickness." He made a sweeping gesture into the air again with his hands. "Bah, sickness. Go away, sickness. I will serenade you." He went off singing one of his Italian tunes at the top of his voice.

"I wish I could get rid of illness as easily," Jack said when Emilio had disappeared into the kitchen. "Just toss it to the wind."

Claire had to agree. "He does have a wonderful way of looking at life, doesn't he?"

"Eat, drink and be merry. Although I don't think it's all goodness and light," Jack went on. "I understand he had a tough time of it back in Italy. He still sends most of his money home to his family."

"You don't see that kind of devotion very often these days." Jack glanced at her. "Meghan's doing well, you know."

She nodded. "I know, and I'm glad. I just wish she were totally well, that she didn't have to have dialysis and that—" She glanced down at the table. "I guess I wish too much."

"You wish that the kidney had worked."

"Yes." She looked back at him. "Yes, I still wish that." She wasn't sure she could ever be reconciled with her disappointment. If the kidney had worked, Meghan would have been on the road to recovery right now, instead of waiting for a transplant.

"It's okay to wish it, Claire," Jack said. "But like I told you before, you can't blame yourself."

"I don't. Not really. Sometimes I wish I could give my other kidney, but then I'd be in trouble, wouldn't I?"

"You wouldn't have any. You know, it's odd," he went on, "since a kidney transplant is virtually the only type of organ transplant that can use a living donor, it has a whole different set of inherent tensions. If it fails you get this guilt complex, like it was such a waste. So many emotions come into play: love, loyalty, fear, resentment."

Claire had felt every one of them. "You make it sound like tossing virgins into the fire."

"In a way it is. Donating an organ, particularly a kidney, is the sacrifice of your own flesh. You have to admit, that's the ultimate sacrifice."

"Now I really feel odd."

"But not like a vestal virgin?"

"Those Romans were rough," she agreed. "Making those ladies tend that fire all those years." She smiled and changed the subject. "Jack, will Meghan be discharged from the hospital when she's stablilized?"

"If we don't get a kidney before then."

"I should start thinking about that, you know. I need to make the arrangements."

"There's no need to do anything just now, Claire. She still has a long way to go. Her blood chemistries aren't exactly what I'd like them to be yet."

"Jack, she's—"

"She's fine, Claire," he cut in. "She's great, in fact. All I said was that her blood work wasn't what I wanted it to be. That doesn't mean she isn't doing well. She's just not doing well enough to leave the hospital."

"I guess I'm overreacting again."

He grinned. "You don't have to apologize. I've been in the same shoes recently."

With her. He'd practically smothered her after surgery. But Claire didn't say anything. Emilio brought out their spaghetti and wine. He set the plates in front of them with a flourish, first hers, "Your favorite, *Signora*—linguine Alfredo."

"You remembered." For some reason, that pleased her.

Always the showman, he continued, "And for the finest doctor in the land, linguine with clam sauce. Just baked, lots of crispy bread—" he put down a basket of garlic bread "—some wine—" a bottle "—and you have

Italian.'' He hesitated a moment, then he said, ''I bring the food, I sing the songs—the love, you must add.''

Claire glanced down at her plate without remarking. Jack didn't comment, either. He thanked Emilio and they ate, enjoying the meal. As always, there was enough for several meals. But it was strange, she felt a tremendous sadness. The Italian must have sensed it, too, for he left them alone. When they got ready to leave, Emilio did hug her again. ''Don't be a stranger,'' he said. ''And bring in the bambino.''

''If it will help make her well, we'll become regular fixtures in here,'' Claire joked.

Jack paid the bill and they went outside. ''Want to go for a walk?'' he asked, zipping up his jacket as the cold air surrounded them. ''It's still early.''

The night was crisp and clear. Claire had gotten used to bundling up and was wearing slacks with her down coat and gloves and boots. ''Why not? Maybe it'll help burn off some of those calories.''

''Emilio is a wonderful cook.''

''Yes.''

''Everything was nice.''

''Yes, very nice.''

''Is something wrong, Claire?''

''No.''

Although silence stretched between them, it wasn't an awkward moment. It was as though they were both comfortable in each other's presence. Still frozen, the snow crunched under their feet as they walked side by side, and she could see their breath in the air, little puffs of steam. Down the block the blue-and-red neon sign denoting the drugstore flashed on and off, the only activity on the block. The street, particularly close to the hospital, was quiet at this time of night. It was as if everyone recognized that the patients were sleeping.

Jack broke the silence at last. "It's a lovely evening."

"Very," Claire agreed. Bright stars studded the inky black sky. Perhaps it was the lack of smog, but the constellations seemed brighter here, closer, almost as if she could reach up and touch them. "The stars are magnificent. I can make out the Big Dipper, but where's the North Star?"

"Over there," he told her, indicating a rather nondistinct spot in the sky.

"It looks so dull."

"It is."

"I always wondered why sailors use it for navigating. It's not particularly bright."

"But it's constant."

Like you, she thought.

"While other stars may move around in the sky, appearing at different longitude and latitude at different times of year," he went on explaining, "the North Star is always in the same place."

"Did you tell Meghan that?"

"Should I?"

"She's fascinated by stars."

They lapsed into another silence. Then Jack spoke as he shoved his hands into his pockets. "By the way, Claire, I know this morning was awkward."

She just shook her head as if the incident were of little consequence. "It was my own fault. I should find out who it is before I open the door."

"That might be a good idea," he agreed. "But I truly didn't mean to embarrass you." They walked a few more steps. Then he said softly, "I meant it when I said you were still beautiful."

"Even with my scar?"

"Particularly with your scar."

"You mustn't have looked very closely, Jack," she teased. "It's pretty ugly and if that's not bad enough, I have stretch marks on my stomach."

"I'd like to see them."

All of a sudden she laughed at the incongruity of their conversation. "I can't believe it," she said. "We're divorced and here we are walking down a street in downtown Minneapolis, and it's ten o'clock at night and at least ten below zero, and we're talking about my stretch marks."

He chuckled along with her. "I don't think things like that are so uncommon, Claire. Besides, if it will make you feel any better, I'm a doctor. I'm supposed to make people feel at ease talking about their private lives."

She wasn't sure that was the entire reason she felt at ease with him. It had more to do with Jack, the person. "You're very special, you know that?"

He seemed surprised by her compliment. He stared at her for a long moment. "Why, thank you."

She laughed again. "I know I'm talking weird. Emilio must have put something in my spaghetti."

"If that's true, I'm glad." They got to the end of the block and rounded the corner. "Except I hope it's something else," he went on.

"Pardon?"

"I haven't made a secret of the fact that I would like for us to get back together, Claire. Or at least, I've wanted us to discuss our differences and see if we couldn't work something out. I've held off because of your surgery. I didn't want to push you."

"And you want to push me now?"

"No. I'm willing to wait, but it's crazy, I feel like we've become friends in the process." The wind had picked up and he pulled her into a vestibule. "Let's talk for a minute."

"In here?" Claire glanced around.

"It's just a doorway," Jack said. "Winos use them all the time."

"Great comparison, Jack. I'll have you know I only had one glass of wine."

He shook his head. "No, I didn't mean that. I did want to explain that I just wanted you to know that I think it's kind of a nice trade-off—being friends. I never knew you before, and you're a nice person."

Perhaps it was the night that begged intimacy between them. Or perhaps it was her surgery or sharing Meghan's illness or not knowing what was going to happen with their child. But Claire felt closer to Jack than she'd ever had. "I think Emilio put something in your spaghetti, too."

His smile was gentle as he slipped her hand in his. "Maybe. But I think it's just us and how we're feeling. Whatever, I like being friends with you."

The vestibule protected them from the elements. Between the stars and the streetlights, it was just bright enough for Claire to see his expression, the blue of his eyes, the jut of his jaw. "And I like being friends with you."

"What is this, a mutual admiration society?"

"I guess. I do admire you, Jack," she said honestly.

Claire couldn't say why, but for some reason the laughter faded. Jack stared at her with something close to anger in his eyes. "I hope you mean that."

"Why?" She frowned at him. "Is something wrong?" They'd been getting along so well.

"Yes," he replied. "Something is wrong. Something is very wrong. It is a mutual admiration society, but I feel like a jerk because all of a sudden it's not admiration I feel for you. And it's sure as hell not friendship."

He wasn't the only one to feel differently. She felt different, too. Weak. Short of breath. But she was far from sick. "What—what *do* you feel, Jack?"

"This." The night had acted as a magical truth serum. Slowly he leaned down to kiss her. Their faces were cold, nipped by the wind and the weather, but his mouth was warm and welcome; soft and sweet and pleasant. She slipped her hands around his neck and drew him closer. Even through their jackets she could feel the heat of his body surrounding her, enveloping her in need.

"Claire," he murmured. "Claire, I need you."

In answer she pressed against him. "Oh, Jack."

Like the last time, he was the one to pull away. He bowed his dark head to her shoulder and gathered control. "Claire, I'm sorry. You know I didn't mean for this to happen." At last he glanced back at her. "I want to be friends with you, Claire. I truly do."

She studied him for a long moment. Then she touched his lips with her mittened fingers. "I want to be friends with you, Jack. But friends feel passion, too, in addition to friendship. And I think it's all right."

"Do you? I hope so."

Two nurses passed by on their way to work. They paused. One of them giggled, recognizing Jack and Claire. "Evening, Dr. Brady."

"Evening," he said.

"Nice night."

"Very." He smiled and took Claire's hand, pulling her from the vestibule. "Come on, I'll walk you back."

They started down the street. Claire couldn't help feeling a bit embarrassed. They'd been necking in the doorway like a couple of kids. "What do you think the gossip's going to be tomorrow?"

"Interesting."

She laughed. What was interesting was how she was feeling about her ex-husband. She wasn't just in love with him. She *liked* him, too. And she couldn't help but wonder where it was all going to lead—and when.

Chapter 9

For the next several weeks Claire made a concentrated effort to relax and recover from her surgery. Although she could technically do almost anything she pleased, she found she grew tired easily and needed lots of sleep. Jack made a concentrated effort to take time off from work, and before she realized it, they were spending more time together than ever before. They would meet each other in the morning at Meghan's bedside and then they would eat dinner together at night—sometimes the two of them at his apartment; other times with Meghan when she felt up to it, in the cafeteria or at his mother's. Roast beef on Sunday became a joke between them.

Claire and Jack had a good time, even with his family. And he kept surprising her with impromptu excursions into the snow: they went for a sleigh ride in the park at least once a week. It was as if once he had gotten her outside into nature, he wasn't going to let her back inside. The night he invited her for a hospital-sponsored

toboggan outing, she was certain she was fully recovered.

"You're sure I'm up to the rigors of a toboggan
chute?" she joked.

Even though he'd encouraged her to do things out of
doors, he'd continued with his overprotectiveness, and he
actually frowned, as though he were a bit worried. "I
thought about that. It's been a month, though, since your
surgery, so you should be fairly safe. Tell you what, I'll
sit in back. You can lean against me. That should serve
as a cushion."

"Jack, I was teasing."

"Oh," he answered. "Well, I wasn't. I don't think we
should bring Meghan. It might be too strenuous for her.
Do you mind?"

"No. Not at all." They'd done a lot with Meghan lately
and from what Claire had heard about tobogganing, it
could be dangerous, particularly since the child had had
a shunt inserted to make access to her blood vessels easy,
and which could dislodge at any time. Besides, more than
likely they would be out late at night.

"I'll meet you up at your room, then," Jack said. "Be
ready."

"Fine." She suppressed a smile as he sailed on down
the hall. He was so accustomed to giving orders. It would
serve him right if she wasn't ready when he arrived.

But she was ready, and surprisingly eager to go. Although it was early March—in *some* cities nearly springtime—it was another cold, clear night. The stars were just
as bright as always. Except for the North Star, which remained in the same spot, constant. Knowing where they
were going, Claire had bundled up. The down coat Jack
had given her was getting quite a workout, and tonight
she'd added her hat.

They drove into the suburbs. Once they'd started to climb, to Claire it seemed higher than the Rocky Mountains. The city was mostly lakes and river and rolling countryside, so the steep hill seemed out of place. Steps had been carved into the snow on the side of the slope, and the toboggan chute entrance was at the top. Every few minutes a sled zipped by, the people screaming and laughing as they went down, down, to the bottom. Huge floodlights illuminated the area, and the hillside looked like a solid glaze of ice.

When they got to the top Jack waved at several people he knew. The crowd stood five or six deep in line, waiting for sleds. "Watch your hands going down, Doc," a laboratory technician joked when they took their places. "One mistake and you won't be able to operate in the morning."

"Operate?" A nurse countered. She'd obviously been down the hill a couple of times. Snow clung to her hat and coat and had crusted on her mittens. "You need to watch your whole body just to stay alive."

Several other people good-naturedly agreed. Although everyone was complaining, Claire noticed they stood in line. She was anxious for their turn. It looked like fun, barreling down a hill at over ninety miles an hour. Jack stood in line beside her and took her hand. When their sled came, he urged her forward. "Come on. Let's go."

As promised, he sat in back. Claire climbed in front of him and leaned into his arms.

"Ready?" he asked.

"Yes."

"Hold on."

It was the inflection in his voice more than anything that set her heart pounding. They were going to fly. As he pushed their sled off the top of the hill with his hands she started to laugh from the sheer fun of it. From this angle the slope looked more than slick. She could see the slight tracks where the snow had been hollowed out in a narrow gorge so that their trip would be a straight run. Straight and fast, until near the end, when the run started to wind around in steep curves. They would have to shift their weight accordingly or be dumped out.

They were almost to the end when Jack shouted at her. "Right! Lean right."

But Claire couldn't move. Although she was leaning against him, the force of the wind held her back. Before she knew it they were face first in the snow, laughing some more.

"You were supposed to lean," Jack told her. They had rolled partway down the hill and he had landed on top of her. The toboggan sat a few yards away.

"I couldn't," Claire answered. "I couldn't move. It was like being paralyzed."

"Hey, Doc, you all right?" someone called.

"We're fine," Jack shouted back.

"You gonna move out of the way?" the voice asked.

"No," he answered, and he grinned down at Claire. "This is more fun."

Claire blushed when it occurred to her how they must look from the top of the hill. She was sprawled in the snow and Jack was lying on top of her. She could feel every inch of him, every hard, firm inch. "Jack?"

"What?"

"This isn't right."

"I think it's great. You're soft."

"You're not. Besides, it isn't polite to lie on top of me."

"So? I don't feel like getting up."

"Oh?" How nice of him. "And why not?"

"I'm comfortable."

She smiled. "No wonder. You're not on the bottom."

All of a sudden he rolled over, taking her with him. She ended up on top of him and he tucked her comfortably between his thighs. "Now I am. Better?"

"No."

"What's the matter?"

She blushed again. "You know what's the matter."

"Okay." He rolled back, pinning her beneath him again. "How about this?"

"Jack, it's the same as before."

He glanced at their positions, gauging the distance. "Really? I thought we were lying over there."

She couldn't help laughing at him. "Lecher. You know darned well if you don't move off of me, people are going to start to talk. We'll be the center of gossip."

"It won't be the first time."

"You're incorrigible, Jack Brady."

"I'd rather be adorable."

"And you're conceited, too." Sticking her tongue out at him, she reached for some snow and shoved it down his back. "There, what do you think about that?"

"It's cold!" he cried as the snow slid down his coat.

"No kidding." Knowing he was going to chase her, and knowing the moment he caught her she was going to get a faceful of snow, she jumped up when he moved, and began to run.

She was no match for him, particularly on the icy hill. He caught her and she tumbled into his arms and they rolled farther down the hill, laughing and rolling and laughing some more. They ended up bumping into a tree near the bottom.

"Oh, Jack, I've never had so much fun in my life," she said when he kissed her lightly on the nose.

"What?" Pausing, he stared down into her eyes. "Fun? In the snow? Claire Brady, California woman, admits to having fun in the snow? In the cold, frozen snow?"

She stuck her tongue out at him again. "You know, Jack, I think there's a mean streak in you."

He laughed. "I'm just shocked, that's all. Say it again."

"I've never had so much fun."

"No. 'I had fun in the snow.'"

"I had fun in the snow."

"Again."

She jumped up and tossed snow at him, chanting, "I had fun in the snow, I had fun in the snow, I had fun in the snow." Then she tucked her hand into his and started up the hill. "Let's go down again."

His pleased laughter rang through the night.

They went down the hill several times. By the third trip, Claire had mastered leaning and they shot the run without overturning. By the fifth or sixth trip, they were experts. When they'd navigated to the bottom again, Jack grabbed her hand and pulled her toward a wooden shelter in the distance. "Come on, Frosty, if you're as tired as I am, you deserve a break. Want some hot chocolate?"

She didn't argue. As much fun as it had been, a respite would be welcome.

The rustic shelter that sat near the toboggan chute served a dual purpose. Half of it was open roofed, serving simply as a shelter. Cold weather enthusiasts could sit on the benches built into the walls or in the logs placed on the ground and enjoy the roaring campfire, away from the wind. The other half was a huge room enclosed by plate-glass windows, so the less hardy could go inside and sit by the fireplace. Either way, people sat around sipping hot chocolate and eating roasted marshmallows.

"Who owns the building?" Claire asked Jack as they walked inside.

"A very smart entrepreneur."

"Also a very wealthy entrepreneur, if all the people are an indication," she added, realizing that half of the hospital staff had to be here.

"The place is rented every night in the winter by one group or another. The hospital tries to arrange an outing several times a season. In the summer, people lease the building for square dances or family functions. It's a gold mine."

"And it's just a hill," she remarked.

Claire unzipped her jacket and took off her hat and mittens as Jack went to a counter and got them both some hot chocolate. He came back carrying two steaming mugs, along with a package of marshmallows and sticks to roast them with.

"Want to sit outside or in?" he asked, balancing everything in his hands.

"Let's go out if you don't mind. We can get near the fire." There were so many people crowded around the fireplace, they'd never get close. She took the hot chocolate from him.

"You must really like roasted marshmallows to brave the great outdoors again."

"I adore them, but your remarks about my aversion to the cold are growing redundant." She gave him a mock angry glare. "Watch it, buster."

"My—" he grinned "—the lady has a temper."

"Just learning that, are you?"

"I'm a little slow." Since he was only carrying the marshmallows, he slung his arm around her shoulders and led her back outside. "Come on, let's eat."

Only a few diehards had gathered around the campfire. There was plenty of room on the log. Since she held their drinks, Jack helped her sit down and then he started fixing their marshmallows.

"Do you like yours cremated or just lightly toasted?"

"Cremated," she answered. "They're mushier inside."

He frowned as if seriously puzzled as he poked a fluffy white treat into the fire. "Tell me, Claire, how did a California girl grow to like marshmallows?"

"We have marshmallows in California," she answered. "They do get shipped to other parts of the country than the snowbelt, you know. When I was a Girl Scout we roasted them all the time."

"Over a stove, I'll bet."

"Of course."

"There's nothing like a marshmallow over a roaring campfire in the cold weather," he said, blowing out the flames and handing her the roasted product.

"Except for sex," someone cut in.

There was a smattering of laughter and someone else answered. "There's only one problem, you get a hot butt."

"The better to sit you with."

The ribald remarks should have embarrassed Claire, but instead she felt pleased when she realized she had been accepted by Jack's co-workers. Ordinarily they would have been reluctant to talk or joke around her, particularly around her and Jack together, and they never mentioned sex in her presence.

"Cool hands."

"Warm bodies."

Claire smiled and shook her head as the banter went on around her. In the meantime Jack had roasted another marshmallow. Although she wouldn't admit these were better, she had forgotten how good they tasted. Along with the hot chocolate and the graham crackers someone handed her, she felt as if she were in sweet heaven. Jack roasted several for himself, too. After they ate, an X-ray technician sitting on the other side of the fire pulled out a guitar and started strumming songs.

"Forget sex," he said. "Let's sing."

For the next hour the group serenaded the countryside. Claire didn't object when Jack leaned back against the log and cradled her in the protective circle of his arms. Two months ago, if someone had told her she would be sitting at a campfire on a night when the temperature hovered near twenty degrees and the windchill factor at below zero, she would have told them they were crazy. Now it seemed like fun. They were hidden from the extreme cold by the shelter; and between Jack and the fire, she wasn't at all chilly, even though they were sitting on the ground. But she was tired, and she yawned.

"Sleepy?" Jack asked.

She nodded, shivering as his breath feathered softly into her ear. "A little. I think it's the marshmallows. They've knocked me out."

"Want to go?"

"If you don't mind."

"No problem." He helped her up from the ground. "I have an early day tomorrow, anyhow. Surgery at dawn." Gathering up the mugs they'd used for hot chocolate, he went on, "I'll just take our stuff inside and be right out."

"I'll be here waiting."

Claire sat on the bench and waited for him, still enjoying the night and the ongoing singing of the campfire contingent. Several people left the building and paused to listen. She wasn't paying attention until she noticed Nancy Ferguson standing nearby, leaning against a wall, her hands tucked into her jacket pockets. Claire had been surprised when Jack mentioned a few weeks ago that the nurse had transferred off his kidney unit. She'd seemed so valuable.

Nancy noticed Claire at about the same time. She smiled, but it seemed forced. "Hello, Mrs. Brady," she said. "You look great. How've you been?"

"Fine, thanks," Claire answered.

"And Meghan?"

"Holding her own." She felt compelled to ask, "How are you?"

"Oh, I'm OK." There was a long, awkward silence. Finally Nancy sighed and said, "How's Jack?"

"Working hard." Claire drew a deep breath. "Do you like your new assignment?"

The nurse shrugged. "I miss the kids sometimes. I'm working a surgical floor, though, so it's not too different. Have you had a good time tobogganing?"

"Yes."

"That's good. I heard you were getting along. Are you going to get back together?"

"Jack and I?"

"No, Jack and the beanstalk." The nurse seemed angry all of a sudden. "You know, it's none of my business, but I hope you don't hurt him again—string him along until Meghan is well and then run back to California."

Claire was stunned by the vehemence in the other woman's voice. "What brought that on?"

"Honesty?"

"You don't think very much of me, do you?" Claire asked.

"No, I don't."

"Why not? What have I done to you?"

"It's nothing you've done to *me*." She gave a short laugh that wasn't a bit humorous. "I love Jack and I don't want to see him hurt."

"You think I'm going to hurt him?"

"I know you are, and it kills me to think about it, because somebody's going to have to pick up the pieces if they can. Jack Brady is a wonderful man and a wonderful doctor, and you have no idea of what hell you're putting him through. Or what hell he's going to go through when you leave." She paused a moment. "Or maybe you do know and just don't care?"

"I care very much," Claire defended herself.

Nancy obviously wasn't convinced. She stepped closer. "Really? Tell me, do you care as much as I do? Do you care enough to take a chance on being hurt? I did." She smiled sadly. "I'm probably crazy for saying this, because I'd like nothing better than to get him back—under any circumstances—but if you care about him then for God's sake tell him so. Give him a chance to be the husband and father he wants to be. Don't keep stringing him along when you don't want him. Don't keep punishing him for something that happened four years ago."

Claire didn't get a chance to answer. When the nurse had finished her speech, she spun on her heel and walked away, disappearing down the hill into the dark night. Jack came out of the building a few moments later, taking Claire by the arm.

"Ready?"

As she turned to him she realized that Nancy was right. He was a wonderful man and a wonderful doctor and she was punishing him. She childishly wanted to hurt him merely because she'd been hurt. Dare she open herself up and tell him how she really felt about him? Without even giving herself a moment to change her mind, she blurted out, "I love you, Jack."

For a long moment he stood there as if he didn't have the slightest idea what she was talking about. Finally he pulled himself together enough to say, "Excuse me?"

She started laughing. She felt as if a giant weight had been lifted from her shoulders. "I said I love you."

"You love— Oh, God."

She reached up to touch his cheek, tracing her fingernail over the fine lines near his eyes. "I love you very much, Dr. Jack Brady. I've never stopped loving you. I love you, I love you, I love you."

He frowned and shook his head, still in a state of disbelief. "I thought— Oh, Claire, I love you, too." Then he scooped her up into his arms and swung her around. "I love you so very much."

They were both slightly delirious, laughing and happy. He set her down and kissed her, soundly, right there, with people singing songs in the background and others milling about. Somebody passed them and whistled, saying, "Go to it, Doc. Better watch your hands, though."

It had to be the laboratory technician.

Someone else laughed. "Must have been some kind of marshmallows."

"Or some kind of toboggan ride," Jack whispered as he released her.

Or an honest nurse, Claire thought.

"Frankly, I don't care what it was," Jack went on, "as long as it's true."

"It's true," she assured him. "I love you." Now that she'd admitted it, she didn't think she would be able to stop saying it. She felt like a broken record, harping on the same line over and over again.

"Then come on, let's go." Taking her hand, Jack turned toward the parking lot. "We've got a lot to discuss."

They drove to his apartment in relative silence. Every time Jack looked at Claire, she would smile, pleased, and he would chuckle. They were both excited. He would take her hand and give it up again to drive. Or he would lean over and kiss her lightly when they pulled up to a stoplight or when traffic bogged down.

"I feel like a kid," he said once, flashing her that special grin of his. "I feel like I've been given the world on a silver platter. Hey, that's a cliché, isn't it?"

"Yes."

"Then how about a bronze platter?"

"Gold," she suggested, kissing him back.

He laughed. "Tell me again."

"What?"

"I love you."

"I love you."

He grinned. "Lord, I love it!"

She laughed. "It's amazing what pleases a person."

"Isn't it?" But he frowned and shook his head. "I didn't think I'd ever hear those words from you, Claire. I thought I'd lost you."

"You did, for a while. But I lost you, too, Jack."

"I think I know where we went wrong," he answered, pulling the car into the parking space by his apartment. "I never took the time to let you learn to like the snow and cold. I just thought you'd accept it, like I had. Only

I didn't stop to think that I'd had close to thirty years in which to do so."

"That might have helped," she agreed. Having had fun in one, she'd certainly changed her mind about the winters. "But that wasn't the most important thing. A great deal of it was my fault, Jack. I was too young for the kind of commitment you wanted. It was very hard for me to understand your priorities."

"Are you saying it's going to be easier now?"

"Not really." She paused, considering, as they entered his building and rode the elevator to his floor. Once they got inside she went on, "I've grown up, but I think being a—" She'd been about to say a doctor's wife, and she caught herself. After all, neither of them had mentioned marriage. "I think being in love with a doctor presents some very serious problems. Maybe I wasn't willing to share you with your vocation before."

He laughed again. "There was nothing to share, Claire. I was never there for you."

But he'd been there for her lately. "Have you made Hal your partner officially?"

"No, but I've delegated a great many of my duties to him." He took their jackets and hung them in the closet. When she took off her hat her hair fell to her shoulders, and she shook it out. "Want something to drink?" he asked.

"I'm fine."

"Sure? I could make some tea."

"No, really, I'm not thirsty. I'm not even cold."

He chuckled, but he sounded uneasy, as if he weren't certain what to do. "Well."

She smiled at him. "What's the matter?"

"Nothing," he said quickly. He gestured around. "I don't know why I came here. We could have talked at Care House."

"It's not as private at Care House."

"No, it's not."

She went into the living room and looked out the window. Every time she came here she was awed by the view. Since he hadn't turned on the lights, the city looked dramatic, the lights stretching for miles and miles into the distance. "It's so clear out. It looks like you could see forever."

"I hear it's supposed to rain. That's why I'm glad the tobogganing party was tonight. The weatherman says we're in a warming trend."

It had been below freezing tonight, but she supposed that wasn't impossible. "A sure sign of spring?"

He laughed. "It can't be far away. This is March. Once we start to warm up, we generally go fast."

He came to stand behind her. Although he didn't touch her, she could feel the heat from his body, the need in him. She turned around. "I love you."

He traced his finger across her lips, along her jaw, down her neck to sift through the silky strands of her hair. "I know. I feel so lucky. I can't believe it. You're so beautiful, Claire. More beautiful than ever."

She really thought she looked awful. She'd just been tobogganing, her cheeks were probably chapped and her hair messed up from the hat she'd worn. The man was too good to be true. Sweet, gentle, considerate. Kind, loving, brilliant. "Jack, do you regret giving over your duties to Hal? Is that why you haven't made him your partner yet?"

"No. I haven't made him my partner yet because I haven't had the time to draw up the papers."

Such a simple answer: no. "Do you think you'll regret it in the future?" She'd hate to think she had made him give up his career.

"No, Claire, I don't think I'll ever regret it. The one thing you've made me realize since you've come back is that medicine isn't the only important thing in my life. You're important to me, Meghan is important to me. We're important to me; we, as a family, me and you and our daughter, we're vital. And I can't replace us with anything—not sick kids or heroics or all the transplants in the world."

Claire bit her lip to keep from crying. She'd run the gamut of emotions tonight, from laughter to excitement to tears, and tears again. How could she ever have doubted him? He was so *kind*! "Oh, Jack, I love you so much."

"I love you, too." He kissed her gently. Then, with a husky groan, he gathered her close. She slipped her arms around his neck and buried her fingers in his thick, dark hair. The moment he touched her, desire surged through her veins, throbbed at her thighs, quickened, tightened her nipples. Jack moved his hands up and covered her breasts, his thumbs circling the erect nipples. Claire moaned deep in her throat and slumped against him, wanting him with every fiber of her being. She wanted nothing more than for him to tear her clothes off and take her right here, on the floor.

But suddenly he drew away and led her to the sofa. She'd thought they were going to kiss some more, perhaps make love. Instead he sat her down and said, "Claire, we need to talk."

His change in mood stunned her. How could he be so serious all of a sudden? Her lips still tingled where he had kissed her, and her body ached for him. Obviously he was just as aroused as she was. She'd felt him against her, the hardness of his need. She drew a deep, calming breath. "What is it, Jack?"

"There are some things we need to discuss, and I want to do it now. In the past we always let passion rule us—we never took the time to talk."

At the moment, talk was the last thing she wanted. In the last few weeks they'd talked each other to death. But considering their past history, they needed to take the time to communicate. "What do you want to talk about?"

"I don't want to hurt you, Claire. I don't know if this is right or if it's wrong. I don't know what it's going to lead to. All I know is that I love you and I don't want to rush you. I don't want this—this moment to happen—unless you do. Oh, hell, I may as well just say it. I brought you here to make love to you."

"I know that, Jack."

"I'm just giving you a chance to say no."

"Do you want me to say no?"

"No. Well, yes, if you want to," he corrected. "I'm really messing things up, aren't I?"

"Yes."

"I just don't want you do anything you'll—"

"Look, Jack," she cut in, taking his hand and kissing his palm lightly. "Will you please just shut up and kiss me?"

That was all the invitation he needed. Tilting her chin up with one finger, he brought his lips slowly to hers. "I thought you'd never ask."

At first he kissed her gently, a mere brush of his mouth across hers. Entwining his hands in her hair, he pressed her back against the sofa cushions and increased the pressure, his mouth hot on hers, hard. Belying their mutual need, he explored her mouth leisurely with his tongue, darting in and out in tiny thrusts, rolling across her teeth. Then all gentleness between them disappeared and it was as if they were back, four years ago, to the time when they couldn't wait. She wasn't certain how they got undressed. They started tugging at each other's clothes, kissing, touching.

Nearly choking with need, Jack crushed her to his body and kissed her almost brutally. Claire didn't mind. She gasped and rocked her hips against his, matching his movements. By now they were both breathing hard and needing release. She'd never wanted anything so badly in her life.

"Claire" was the only thing Jack said to her as he trailed a path along her heated skin with his mouth. His hands were everywhere at once, on her breasts, teasing the swollen peaks, trailing down her stomach, drawing circles on the insides of her thighs, finally pausing in her moist warmth. He kissed her all over, too, his mouth and tongue working magic on her heated skin.

"I love you," she murmured, meeting him touch for touch, stroke for stroke.

"You're sure?"

"Yes. Love me, Jack."

And then she was lost in the maelstrom as he entered her and began a slow, tortuous rhythm in and out, in and out. With each movement the tempest within her gathered strength, raging into an uncontrolled whirlwind of passion, of need. She felt as though she'd been bruised and battered by its intensity. It whirled through her with tremendous force, spiraling, thundering toward its peak. Though it was cold she was damp with sweat. Jack's body was slippery. At the height of desire, she cried out and clutched his arms as he held her, wanting more and yet needing to pull away because the pleasure was so intense. She gasped as she crested the zenith and for a moment the earth ceased to move. The only things that existed in the universe were the moon and the stars and Jack. He became the source of her being; and then contentment rippled through her in waves.

It took him a few moments to move from her. When he could gather the strength, he rolled over, pulling her with him and resting her head on his shoulder. With a sigh, he brushed back her sweat-dampened hair and kissed her forehead gently. "Kind of wild, huh?"

"I believe it was a bit more rigorous than a toboggan chute," she answered, trying to get her breath back.

"Are you all right?"

An odd question. She felt wonderful. "I'm fine Why?"

"I didn't mean to hurt you."

"I'm fully recovered," she reminded him.

"Not quite fully." She was lying, turned to her side, half on, half off him. He traced his finger along the scar on her flank. "It'll be a couple more weeks yet. I guess I've been hovering again, haven't I?"

"Very much." It was odd lying here talking to him without her clothes on. They had just shared the most intimate moment a man and woman can experience, and she felt easy being with him.

He continued to trace her scar, rubbing his finger along it almost absently. Then he paused and said, "You know how much I admire you for this, don't you?"

"Giving my kidney to Meghan?" She switched her position, resting her hand on his chest and tucking her chin on it to glance up at him. "I've told you before, it was no big deal, Jack. What you do—operating, saving lives—that's a big deal."

"I'm glad you think so." He smiled and went back to her scar. "Hal did a nice job."

"If you consider a huge purple slash a nice job, then yes, he did a nice job."

That made Jack laugh. "How about your stretch marks? Are they equally as lovely?"

"Gorgeous."

"You know, you women have a way of wearing your courage," he went on. "We men aren't so lucky."

"Having a baby takes courage?"

"A lot. Particularly when you're alone and bleeding."

"Oh, Jack, you don't have to apologize," she said softly, realizing he was feeling guilty over what had happened. "I've gotten over that. I truly have."

He leaned down and kissed her lightly on the nose. "You're a brave woman, Claire."

"If you keep telling me that, I'm going to get a swelled head."

"Hmm," he remarked, "and if we keep lying here I'm going to get a swelled something else."

"Really?" She smiled at him. It wasn't too often he made sexual innuendos. "And what might that be?"

"Don't make me say it."

She laughed huskily. "Tell me, Dr. Brady, what time are you due back at the hospital?"

"Tomorrow morning. Why?"

"Because I think we should lie here—" she tiptoed her fingers along the dark hair that arrowed down his stomach, down, down, until she touched him intimately "—and talk—" he gasped, hitching his breath in as she softly enunciated the rest of the sentence "—all night long."

Chapter 10

"What do you want to do—all night long?" Jack asked huskily.

"Well..." Claire pretended to think. "For starters I've never seen your bedroom. You could show me your sheets. Maybe we could have that tea you offered to make earlier. We could talk some more. Or you could take my previous advice and shut up and kiss me."

"I'm not the one talking."

She wrinkled her nose. "Kiss me anyhow."

"You're being awfully forward tonight, aren't you?"

"Definitely out of character," she murmured, continuing to tease him by twirling her finger in tiny circles across his abdomen. "But as I recall, you always made me this way. Do you want me to stop?"

"No." He caught his breath as she touched him intimately again, drawing little circles there, too. "No, I don't want you to stop." When she trailed her fingernail up and down his length, he grabbed her and pulled her from the sofa. "Come on, let's take a look at the bedroom. You're right. It's time I showed you my sheets."

They made love again. To Claire, the first time had been wonderful. This time was equally as exquisite. She felt as if she had been given a gift too precious for words, and in a way she had—a gift of him. They had given each other the ultimate bond: a part of themselves. Though she had made love with him many times, the act never ceased to awe her.

Afterward she placed her head on his shoulder and curled up next to him. As he stroked his hand absently through her hair they lay awake talking, sharing intimacies, recalling moments from the past. She complimented him on his bedroom, which was as tasteful as the rest of the apartment and decorated in much the same way. The sheets were red, but they were cotton. That amused her because instead of being silk and daring, they were practical, like him. The only impractical items in the room were a huge jade elephant that reared his trunk in the corner, and a set of fancy swords that crisscrossed behind the bed.

"Are they to ward off evil spirits?" she asked, eyeing the sharp tips.

"No, a patient gave them to me. He was a collector. They seemed to fit in with the decor, so I put them behind the bed."

"They would certainly scare off any lady friends."

"No lady friends have seen them," he said, raising himself up to look at her. "Except you."

She'd been teasing, but she could tell from his expression that he wasn't. "I'm sorry, Jack. That's really none of my business."

"Yes, it is." He seemed so serious, so intense, his forehead wrinkled in a concerned frown. "Claire, I want you to know that Nancy and I never made love here."

"Oh." What was she supposed to say? *Golly, gee, I'm glad. I hate to follow other women in bed.*

Yet in a way his admission did make her feel better. She would have hated lying in the same bed another woman had been in. She would have wondered what side she'd lain on, and if she'd stretched languorously afterward, as Claire had.

She took a deep breath. "But you did make love?"

"No I was never in love with her. But we did come pretty close."

"I see."

"I don't think you do. I'm sorry, Claire." His voice was haunted, pained; and yet, strangely, the hurt was for her and not for himself. "I wouldn't hurt you for the world, but I didn't think you were coming back. I didn't think we would ever be together again."

"It's all right, Jack," she murmured at last. He was human, after all, and they'd been divorced.

"Is it?" He tilted her chin so that she was looking at him. "I'm not sure. Do you see it as a betrayal?"

"No, not really," she said, knowing she was speaking the truth. While one part of her was hurt, the other part of her had to be realistic. She'd left Jack, and she'd made it clear she didn't want to see or talk to him again. What was he supposed to do? "I'd like to think that all this time you didn't want anyone else but me," Claire went on. "But I know she loved you, and that makes it easier. Despite everything, I like her. She's a wonderful person. Sometimes I feel guilty for coming back and spoiling things for her. She was there tonight, you know, tobogganing." Claire paused. "She made me realize that if I loved you, I had to tell you. She made me realize I had to take a chance.''

"She spoke to you?"

"Yes, while you were inside, returning the mugs.''

"I'm sorry."

"Don't be. She was right.''

"There will be someone for her, Claire," Jack said. "I know she'll meet someone. She knew how I felt from the beginning.''

"But I'm sure she had hopes. I know when I met you that's what I had.''

He laughed and twirled a lock of her hair around his finger. "When you met me you weren't doing anything but bleeding, Claire Brady. You didn't even open your eyes and look at me until I got your finger sewed up. And then I had to act like a fool to get your attention.''

"Is that what you call what you were doing? Here I thought you were being charming.''

"I had to practically stand on my head to get you to go out with me that night.''

"That's only because I was weak from the loss of blood," she said in a long-suffering tone. "After I got stronger I was fine. We even made love," she reminded him.

"Yes, I remember." He kissed the tip of her nose. "I'll always believe that was the night you got pregnant with Meghan.''

After that they'd made love so often the actual date had been hard to determine. "It probably was," she agreed. "Poor Meghan, conceived in the back seat of a car.''

"Front seat."

"That leaned back into the back seat, making a bed," she corrected. They'd gone to the movies in an old Nash

Rambler that he'd borrowed from a friend. "Whatever happened to that car?"

"John traded it in on a Mercedes the day he finished his residency."

"It's kind of hard to make love in a Mercedes."

"You would have to be determined."

"You know," she went on curiously, "I haven't seen a Nash Rambler in years."

"Good thing."

"Jack!"

He chuckled and drew her close. "I thought about buying it from John as a memento, but you'd left me, and I really didn't want to drive the darned thing."

It was so old no one would, except maybe an antique car buff or a teenager who wanted to impress his girl-friends.

"How about you? Has there been anyone since me?"

"No."

"I'm glad." He touched her finger where she had worn her wedding band.

She paused and studied him a moment—the dark hair, the blue of his eyes. He was the kindest, most sincere man she'd ever met. "What happened to us, Jack? Where did we go wrong?"

Although she'd asked the question, Claire didn't really expect an answer. For her part, she knew what had happened. For his part, too. What she was expressing was regret, based on a moment of whimsy. They'd been so happy together.

He must have understood. "I wish I knew. I think you were right before, when you said we were too young. And we really didn't know each other, either," he went on. "But the important thing is, we've found each other again."

"Only at what price? Meghan's sick."

"Meghan would have gotten sick whether or not you left me, Claire. Don't harbor guilt over that."

"You might have noticed it sooner."

"I doubt it. You got her in right away."

"I suppose." She hated her child being sick; even more she hated being helpless. "Sometimes I wonder why things happen a certain way. You know what they say— things happen for a reason. I just wonder what reason."

"That's probably true, things do happen for a reason, but believe me, Claire, Meghan didn't get kidney disease so you would come back to me. She got kidney disease because something went wrong with her filtration system. If anything, consider us lucky that she got sick now, when there's so much equipment and so many modern advances at our disposal to help treat her. It's hard to imagine, but less than twenty years ago they were doing dialysis in old washing-machine tubs."

Considering the sophisticated equipment they hooked Meghan up to three times a week, it *was* hard to imagine. "Thank you for trying to make me feel better."

"I'm not just saying it, Claire. I mean every word."

She kissed his cheek. "I know, and I love you for it."

They lay silent for a long moment. "Sure you don't want to go back to Care House tonight?" Jack asked. "I know how you feel about gossip, and I'll be glad to take you."

For once she didn't care about gossip. She glanced at the clock on the bedside table. She'd have to get dressed, and she was tired. Not operation tired, but love tired. Sated. And she was comfortable with him—comfortable here. There was no reason to return. Jack had called the nurse at the desk to inquire about Meghan and sometime during the night it had started raining. She could hear the drops on the windowpanes and on the street below. The cars driving through the puddles. The warming trend must have started. Soon it would be spring.

"We'll get back early, won't we?" she asked. "I don't want to miss breakfast. Meghan ordered oatmeal for us both."

"Oatmeal?" He made it sound like a sin.

"It's good for you."

"If you say so. To answer your question: yes, we'll be back early. I have surgery at dawn."

"Fine. Let's stay here."

"I was hoping you'd say that," He drew her back into his arms, tucking her body close to his. "I wanted to share the night with you—the entire night," he added. "I love you, Claire."

She snuggled closer to him, content to be cradled in his arms. The rain had picked up. In the distance she could hear thunder; not loud, just soft, distant. Thunder in the winter—she'd heard some kind of saying about it somewhere, but she couldn't recall what it was. She frowned, trying to remember, when the phone rang. How many times had it interrupted their marriage?

Jack glanced at the bedside table. "I wonder who that is?"

"The hospital, probably." Claire leaned up on one elbow and pushed her hair out of her eyes.

"Maybe I should ignore it. I am off duty."

"You don't have to ignore the phone because of me," Claire told him, suddenly realizing that was the reason he was hesitating. "I've learned not to be selfish these days. I can share you with anyone."

"Feeling righteous, are you?"

"Actually, yes," she said. "I think the difference is that you're not so anxious to go anymore."

He frowned. "Strange logic."

"But true." She nodded to the bedside table. "Jack, if you don't answer soon, they're going to hang up."

He sighed and reached for the phone. "I suppose."

Although he had procrastinated, he became immediately alert and interested the moment he picked up the phone. He sat up on the side of the bed and grabbed a pen. Claire had been lounging in the bed watching him, when he set the pen back down and listened for a moment. Her heart sank as she watched a multitude of emotions play across his face: fear, dread, anxiety—hope. When he spoke, his words were grave. "Did you call Hal? Get everything ready, I'll be right there."

It didn't take a genius to know something was wrong. Claire sat up and clutched his arm. To think that only moments ago she'd felt content, comfortable, curled in his arms. "Oh, God. What is it, Jack?"

"It's Meghan," he said.

She felt her heart lurch. Earlier, she'd thought she'd run the gamut of emotions. She had no idea she would be juggling one more: fear. "No! Please—"

"She's fine. Claire, there's a kidney," he finished. "We've got to hurry."

"A kidney?" She came alive. "Oh, Lord, a kidney! I don't believe it." He didn't need to add anything more. She jumped out of bed and started throwing on her clothes as quickly as he donned his. "When? What happened?"

"Just a few minutes ago. I have to go with the team to pick it up," he told her as they both rushed around the room getting dressed. "They're doing the surgery to remove it right now. In the meantime they're going to prep Meghan for surgery and find Hal."

They'd waited for this moment. Meghan had been on the list for weeks, but now that her chance had arrived, Claire was petrified. So much could happen. She'd been through one failed transplant. Now she might have to face another one. She knew from experience there was a lot to do.

"You mentioned you had to pick up the kidney," Claire said. "Was it an accident?"

"I don't have all the details, but I understand it's from a little girl who was killed in a car wreck earlier tonight. Her parents just signed the papers, and Meghan was matched to her as soon as possible."

"The other kidney?"

"They matched it to a young boy in Michigan."

Claire felt sad known a child had died. At the same time she had a hard time controlling her feeling of elation. She wanted to jump up and down for joy. Meghan was getting a kidney. Her daughter was getting another chance at life. But it was all so dangerous. So chancy. One moment she was down, scared, the next she was up, joyous. "How far away?"

"Chicago. It should only take us a few hours to get the organ and be back. We'll work quickly."

She wanted to ask more, but even if Jack happened to have the details, they didn't have time to talk. They were both dressed and they headed out the door in minutes. Although it was raining, the drive to the hospital was quick, silent, as they both thought about the events yet to come. All Claire could think of was the end result. The windshield wipers flipped back and forth, back and forth, as she clung to the only thing she had: hope, precious hope. It was pitch-dark out, barely three in the morning. The moon and stars had disappeared.

When they pulled into the parking space Jack took her hand. "We're going to make it through this, Claire," he said softly. "This time we're going to make it, and the kidney's going to work."

"I know," she said. But she *didn't* know. She didn't know what to think or what to do or what to want. "I'll be okay, Jack. You don't have to worry about me."

"But you have doubts?"

"Don't I always?"

"Doubts are good, Claire," he said. "They keep us human. Just don't let them consume you. Are you going to call your mother?"

She nodded. "I think I'd better at least let her know. I'll call your mother, too, if you'd like."

"Thank you. For the most part I'll be with the surgical team, and I won't have a chance to contact her. She'll want the news." He turned his attention back to Claire. "Are you going to be all right? Would you rather I stay with you? Hal can go for the kidney."

"No," she said emphatically. "I want you to do it. I'll be with Meghan."

"What about during surgery? I can be with you then."

She shook her head again. In that instant she knew she truly could share him. Although temporarily, she could always give him up to his patients in the name of love. "I want you where you belong, Jack, in that operating room with our daughter." Now, more than ever, she appreciated his skill and dedication. "I want Meghan to have the best chance there is, and that's with you."

He smiled that gentle grin of his that told her he'd do his best. "That's quite a compliment."

"All true."

"I appreciate your confidence." He actually sounded cheerful. How could he always be so optimistic? Claire wondered, as he let go of her hand so they could get out of the car.

The kidney unit was a flurry of activity when they got inside the hospital. The lights at the nurses' station were ablaze and the entire surgical team had been assembled, each of them attending to their particular duties. Someone was checking the perfusion pump, another person packed medical supplies. The helicopter pilot had a weather report. Jack squeezed her hand and gave her a quick kiss goodbye before he joined the people milling about at the nurses' desk.

"I'd like to stop in to see Meghan just before we leave. The surgery will take place just as soon as I get back. Hal's staying here to have Meghan ready. They won't wake her until it's time to go down. I won't be able to see her before surgery. When I get back I'll go directly to the O.R."

"Jack, you don't have to explain," she said.

"I just don't want you to worry, Claire."

"That's like saying you don't want me to breathe."

He smiled. "I guess that's true. Okay, breathe, but not too deeply."

She pushed him toward the nurses' station. "Go."

When Jack left to join the crew, Claire went to her daughter's room, tiptoeing in and settling quietly into a chair. She didn't want to wake either of the girls. Kathleen and Meghan were both sound asleep. She wondered if Meghan was dreaming. She slept so peacefully, clutching her teddy bear in her arms, her eyelashes so very dark where they rested on her pale skin. Soldier had been through as much as the child. He had Band-Aids all over his body, placed there by an understanding staff. Now he'd have a kidney, another Band-aid.

Kathy was smiling, probably thinking of a boy—or about the new intern she'd been eyeing. Would Meghan ever get to be a teenager? Claire didn't want the doubts to seep in. She wanted to be positive, but she couldn't prevent her fears. What if her child died? What if the kidney didn't take again? It seemed as if she were constantly asking herself that question. Unfortunately she still hadn't come up with an answer.

A few minutes later, as the surgical team went down the hall to the elevator, Jack stopped in the room. As though not wanting to wake Meghan, either, he tiptoed to her bedside and leaned down on one knee to kiss her gently on the cheek. He didn't say much more to Claire when he got up. He took her hand and squeezed it tightly as he brushed his lips with hers. "I'll be back as soon as possible. Hang in there."

She nodded.

"This is a time for joy, Claire. Everything's going to be all right." He kept trying to console her. "Trust me."

"I do."

And oddly she did. Jack would do everything he could, if not more. But with the last operation she had learned that there were so many variables, so many dangers.

After he left, Claire went to the phone and called his mother and then hers. Angeline Brady quickly arrived at the hospital. Jack's mother didn't say much; she just hurried into Meghan's room and glanced down at her sleeping grandchild. Then she came to sit by Claire.

The two women didn't speak. They didn't have to. Claire knew without Angeline's saying so, that his mother understood every single fear Claire felt, simply because she was a mother too. They held hands.

"Do you want me to call your mother?" Angeline asked.

"I already did, thanks."

"It's going to be all right, Claire."

Everyone seemed to think so. Claire wished she was as easily convinced. "Thanks."

Jack was gone longer than he'd predicted. The rain didn't let up. Dawn rose over the horizon cold and gray, the leaden skies matching Claire's mood. As soon as the day shift arrived, someone woke Meghan and began to get her ready for surgery. Although Jack still wasn't back, they had to have Meghan in the operating room, ready for the transplant the moment the kidney arrived.

The child was excited, caught up perhaps by the hurried mood of the staff. Everyone rushed around drawing blood, running laboratory values, getting her ready for surgery. As before, she didn't show any fear. But then she was so young—too young to know the risks. Kathleen seemed to think it all a great bore. She had yet to receive a kidney, and considering her other complications, might not get one for several more months. Yet when it came time for Meghan to be taken down to the surgical suite, Kathy waved a goodbye.

"See you later, kid," she said. "I'll keep the television hot for us."

"Okay," Meghan agreed, hugging her teddy bear. "I'll be back." She glanced at Claire. "And then I'm gonna have a kidney that works. Right, Mommy?"

"Right," Claire answered.

"And then I'm gonna go home. Right?"

"Yes, honey. Just as soon as your kidney's working, you're going to go home."

Claire leaned down to kiss her child, hoping it would all come true. But when they wheeled the cart away she felt as if part of her heart were being ripped from her body. She couldn't speak. She could hardly move. She stood there in the hallway, waving to her daughter and smiling through her tears.

Jack's mother took her hand and squeezed again.

"Oh, God, I can't stand it," Claire said. "I love her so much." The only thing stronger was her love for Jack.

"I know." His mother patted her back. "I know you do."

The two women waited in a private waiting room right outside the surgical suite. Although it was a comfortable area with sofas and chairs, Claire didn't notice. She sat on the edge of a chair staring straight ahead and wondering what was happening. She didn't know a thing about operations except what had happened to her, and she kept imagining every step of what they were doing to Meghan. First they would transfer her to an operating table. The doctor would joke with her. Another doctor would come in and try to make her feel at ease. They would lean over the table looking funny in their masks and caps and gowns.

Would Meghan think it was funny?

Claire stood up and paced to the window across the way. Someone brought in coffee and rolls. She looked at them, acknowledging the food, but she didn't take either. She wished she knew if Jack were back.

"Claire, you should try to relax," his mother said to her at last. She had just paced to the window for probably the hundredth time.

"I can't."

"You're going to be a nervous wreck."

"I'm worried."

"There's nothing you can do but wait."

"I guess I'm not very patient." She knew the woman was right. She tried to think of another subject. "Have you ever had to wait like this?"

"Oh, yes, many times."

Claire smiled. "All those grandchildren?"

"That, and Mr. Brady had surgery a couple of times. He had a heart attack once."

That's how much attention Claire had paid to Jack's family. "Father Brady?"

"Yes, when the kids were much younger. When Jack had his tonsils out, I waited for hours."

"Was he a child?"

"He was just a little guy. My little guy."

He wasn't so little anymore. He was all grown up, a man now, but Meghan was tiny—tiny and helpless. Tears sprang to Claire's eyes. She wasn't ordinarily so emotional, but she couldn't help it today. "I wish—thank you for being here with me," she said gently.

"Oh, Claire." The older woman got up and took Claire into her arms again. "There, there, don't cry."

Claire took a deep breath and wiped her eyes. She was overreacting and she knew it. They probably hadn't even given Meghan the anesthesia yet. "I'll be all right."

"I wish you would have let your own mother come."

Claire gave a half laugh. "I would have been worse. My mother and I have the same emotional disposition."

"You may think you're weak, Claire, but you're strong. You're the strongest woman I've ever known."

She was stunned. Coming from his mother that was a supreme compliment. "Thank you."

"You're welcome. You know, in a way, I'm glad all this has happened," his mother went on saying. "We've really gotten to know each other."

"Yes, we have," Claire agreed. She'd gotten to know Jack, too. Maybe things did happen for a reason. Odd, earlier she'd gone tobogganing and she'd enjoyed it. Odder still, she was sitting here letting Jack's mother comfort her. If anyone had told her three months ago she would be friends with Jack's mother, Claire would have thought them crazy. Now she was depending on the woman for support. But she supposed things changed, people changed, grew, were molded by their experiences.

But what an experience!

Sybil found them a few minutes later. Claire hadn't seen her friend in a couple of days. When the Montana woman walked into the room, she was delighted.

"Sybil!"

"Hi there." Sybil grinned. "Hey, I caught you dressed for a change. I hear Meghan's in surgery."

"How did you know?" Claire was surprised. Everything had happened so fast.

"Nancy Ferguson called me."

Claire shook her head in amazement. "I'm beginning to think that woman's a saint."

"They all are around here, Claire. It's a requirement for hiring. I hear she's leaving town. She got a job at the new kidney unit they've opened in Detroit, and she was packing, but when she heard about Meghan, she remembered you and I were friends and thought I'd want to be with you. I found a ride for Robbie to get to school and came right over."

"I just hope this works," Claire answered.

"It will. Remember: never give up hope. I thought I'd wait with you if you don't mind."

"I'd be delighted. How's Robbie?" She felt bad for not having asked before.

"Fine. We're still waiting for a kidney. He's got that rare blood type. Complicates matters."

"We're lucky."

Sybil agreed. "Yes, I'd say you are. Damn lucky, in fact. I hear you and Jack are getting along."

Claire nodded, not even caring that his mother could hear. "We're doing all right. We've talked some."

"Getting back together?"

Claire blushed, embarrassed. "I don't know about that."

"If he did ask you, would you marry him again?" his mother asked abruptly.

Claire paused before she answered. She hadn't thought that far ahead. They'd managed to reconcile some of their differences but they hadn't discussed the future. What it all really boiled down to was how she felt, and she felt at home here. This was where she belonged, with her husband and child. "Yes. I'd marry him again."

"I'm glad. I was afraid you wouldn't. I was afraid I'd messed things up forever."

Now Claire went to hug his mother, who had started to cry. "Everything's okay, Mrs. Brady. Please don't cry."

His mother laughed though her tears. "I'm supposed to be comforting you."

"I'm glad we're comforting each other."

"A crisis does funny things to people," Sybil spoke up. "It makes friends of enemies and enemies of friends."

Claire had to nod agreement. In this case, the crisis had helped her not only mend her fences with her mother-in-law, but rediscover the man she loved.

She never found out exactly when Jack returned to the hospital with the kidney. People bustled in and out of the surgery suite constantly, but no one came to the waiting room. An hour passed. Then two. The women talked, discussing knitting, the weather, whatever they could think of to pass the time. Finally Claire got up and went to the window to look out. It was barely eight o'clock in the morning.

Just when she was least expecting it, Jack swept into the room still wearing his green surgical scrubs. From the sweat that dampened his cap and shirt, Claire could tell he'd been in the operating room for a long time. Both Sybil and his mother stood up, expecting him to make a happy announcement, but all he did was shake his head and say, "I don't have any news yet except that she's made it through surgery. They're closing the incision now. I came to tell you because I knew you were worried."

She was almost afraid to ask. The words came out in a whisper, "The kidney?"

"I don't know. They'll tell us as soon as they can."

"Does that mean it's taken?"

"Yes. Everything went fine. It's a good, healthy kidney."

There could be several complications down the road—rejection, infection—but this was the first hurdle. Without a functioning kidney it would all have been for nothing. Jack stood beside Claire, folding her into his arms. At first she thought he was giving her his strength, then she realized he needed her, and she wrapped her arms around his waist and held him tightly. Sensing that Jack and Clair needed the time alone, Sybil and his mother left the room.

"She made it through the surgery," he said gently as they stood there rocking back and forth, holding each other. "That's all we can hope for at the moment, Claire. Give it a little time.

"I have. I've given it weeks, months."

"It won't be long till we know."

Since he seemed to have collected himself, she turned from him and glanced back out the window. For the past few minutes she'd been looking out at the snowman that Meghan had built before the first surgery, the same snowman Claire had repaired the day she'd been discharged. The rain had almost completely melted it. The red scarf she had tied around the neck at such a jaunty angle was a soggy mess hanging from a white blob. In a way it was again symbolic, since it reflected their plight. They'd done everything they could. She'd given her kidney. Jack had given his expertise. Now it was up to nature and God to determine their child's fate.

"The snowman's gone," she said to Jack.

Coming to stand beside her again, he glanced out the window. "Actually, it's amazing it stayed for this long."

"I suppose. Did you find out about the little girl who died?"

"Do you really want to know? Sometimes that information can become a burden."

The psychiatrist she had seen had warned her along with every other patient he counseled against getting too involved with the donor's family; it wasn't healthy. Simply accept it and go along. "I just want to thank them," Claire said.

"I already did."

"Good. Will I be able to see Meghan soon?"

"They'll be taking her to the recovery room as soon as Hal's done. I'll visit her there and see if the kidney's working."

"We'll know that soon?"

"I told you: any moment now."

Just then a nurse bustled into the room. She was smiling. "Dr. Brady? Dr. Davies asked me to find you. He thought you might want to know the kidney's working. Everything's fine."

Claire hadn't realized just how tense Jack had been. Relief flooded through him visibly. "Thank God," he murmured. Then he smiled at her and held out his arms. She went into them naturally, as if she'd belonged there always, as if she'd never left. Once again he said, "Thank God."

Chapter 11

Claire sat at Meghan's bedside most of the day. Sybil left for work as soon as the child came from the recovery room and they determined that she was all right. Jack's mother stayed until early afternoon. After she left, his relatives came in a steady stream, one at a time, offering support, encouragement, a pat here, a squeeze there, a whispered word, a nod. Even his father visited, crying. How could she ever have missed seeing the love they gave so openly and freely?

Jack still had several scheduled surgeries but he came in and out whenever he could. Meghan slept a lot. When the child woke she wanted to know about her kidney. "Yes, honey, this one took," Claire told her.

"Did Soldier's kidney take?"

As a way to reassure the children, whatever the staff did to Meghan, they "did" to her teddy bear, too. Soldier had a huge Band-Aid over his abdomen in the same place Meghan had been operated on, signifying the transplant. "Yes, his took, too. It's working just fine."

Meghan smiled happily. She drifted off to sleep, hugging the stuffed animal. Before Claire knew it, night had fallen. Jack came into the room looking as exhausted as she felt, if not more so. He checked Meghan's chart and examined the child closely. Then he kissed her goodnight, pushing a stray lock of dark hair from her face. "She's such a beautiful child," he said.

Claire glanced at their daughter. "She takes after you."

"Not totally." He smiled. "She's got your disposition."

"Sweet?"

"Not totally," he repeated. "Ready to go?"

"Where?"

"To my place. We both need some rest."

Claire wanted to stay at the hospital. "Do you think Meghan will be all right alone? I'm not sure we should leave her. She's so little."

"She'll be fine, Claire. She's doing great, and the nurses will call us at the slightest change. Besides, we need to get some sleep before we keel over, and we need to get away from here for a while. For once, I'm taking my own advice and going home to rest."

Claire had forgotten that neither of them had slept for two days. "Are you off duty again?"

"Hal's taking my calls."

"He's going to get tired of these nights, you know," she said, teasing him.

He nodded. "I've really been giving him the bad hours. But it all evens out in the end. Come on." He put his arm around her shoulder and steered her toward the door. "We'll come back early in the morning. I ordered you a breakfast tray, complete with oatmeal."

"Can Meghan eat tomorrow?"

"No, but I didn't want you to miss out on your favorite."

"Gee, thanks. I'll have you know I only eat it because of Meghan."

"Oh, sure. I get those stories all the time. Usually it's the frosted cereal, though, that people crave."

"I'm weird."

Jack didn't comment. Because she knew he would never leave unless Meghan was stable, Claire didn't object when he led her away. She put her arm around his waist and walked with him down the hall.

"I talked with Hal about a partnership finally," he said as they got on the elevator and rode down.

"Today?" With all he had to do?

"We happened to be scrubbing side by side for surgery. It seemed an opportune moment."

"And?"

"He was thrilled. We're going to have papers drawn up and then we're in business."

"It's that easy, huh?"

"Amazing. I should have done it four years ago."

"Four years ago you were a resident," she reminded him. "You couldn't take a partner."

"But if I could have, maybe things would have been different."

"I don't think so, Jack," she told him. "What happened between us was as much my fault as yours."

"You know, when you first came here we argued over whose fault it was, too."

They'd claimed just the opposite, though, blaming each other. "Are we arguing?"

"Talking."

"Sounds more like arguing to me." He had a thing about talking these days. Ever since they'd determined that communication had been a problem between them, it was as if he were going to talk her to death.

"Talking. Always talking. I love you," he said.

She glanced up at him. "Me, too."

He leaned down to kiss her just as the doors slid open to the first floor. A crowd of people waited to get on, but Jack didn't seem to mind. Slinging his arm around her shoulder, he grinned at everyone and said, "Good evening."

"Good job, Jack," a fellow doctor spoke up. He tipped his head to Claire. "Mrs. Brady."

Claire assumed he was talking about the operation on Meghan, but she wasn't certain, even when Jack nodded and answered, "Thanks."

"Going home?"

"Yes."

"It's about time," the man said as the doors slid closed again.

"I agree." Jack turned Claire toward the front door.

Surprisingly the rain hadn't let up at all. Claire covered her head with her hands and started to run alongside Jack, splashing her way to his car. "This is awful. Is it what always happens during a warming trend?"

"Pretty much," he answered. "If you think this is bad, wait until the spring rains. Some people even start to build arks."

They made it to his car and to the apartment without getting too awfully soaked. Once they were inside and he'd closed the door, though, Claire shivered from the cool air. Jack shook out their coats and hung them over the backs of chairs to dry, right on the expensive carpet. As he handed her a towel to fluff her hair, he went into the kitchen to put on water. "I'll make some bouillon. It'll help relax us."

Claire kicked off her shoes and followed him, yawning hugely. "If I get any more relaxed, I'll be a zombie."

"Just don't fall asleep yet. If I remember right, you snore."

She arched an eyebrow at him. "How ungallant of you to recall such a thing. Anyway I snore because I'm tired," she defended herself self-righteously.

"Actually, I don't care if you snore or not," he said. "I want to hold you before you go to sleep. If you drop off now, I'll have to carry you to bed and leave you to it."

"Oh, terrific."

It was terrific, and it made her heart melt, the way he expressed it. But Claire didn't have to say so. She had a feeling Jack knew. He made the bouillon and set a steaming mug in front of her. "Want to go in the other room?"

"To get comfy on the sofa? Sounds good, but I'd better not. I already told you I was in danger of falling asleep at any moment. And I don't want to snore." She couldn't help getting in the last word. She leaned her elbow on the counter and placed her chin on her hand. "So, what's the point of the bouillon?"

He shrugged. "I don't know. I just wanted to have bouillon with you. We used to drink it, you know. You'd have some ready for me when I came home."

She nodded, remembering. And then they'd make love.

"We have some good memories, Claire."

"Yes. And some bad ones, too," she said honestly. After Meghan was born their routine had changed. She'd been busy with a baby; he'd been busy learning to be a doctor. "Jack," she said abruptly, "how long do you think the kidney's going to last?"

"Meghan's? I have no way of knowing. Why?"

"Sybil told me a long time ago there was only a five-year survival rate."

"Yes, that's true. But it could last longer—it could last forever, for that matter."

"How will we know?"

"We'll watch her closely. Claire, Meghan isn't cured," he went on seriously. "I thought you knew that. We talked about it before. She's got a long road ahead of her. She could reject the kidney, or she could get an infection. Anything could happen. It could work fine for three years or five, or fifteen, and then all of a sudden stop. I can't say with any accuracy what the future will hold. We just have to deal with it one day at a time, and rely on our skills."

"That seems so depressing."

"How could it possibly be depressing?" he asked. "She has a kidney. She's not dependent on machines. She has us. We love her. We love each other."

"But she's not like a normal child."

"No, she's not," he agreed. "But that's no big deal. As long as we watch her for complications, she'll be fine."

Claire stirred her bouillon thoughtfully, thinking of all the things she wanted for her child. "Can she have a normal life? Can she grow up and get married and have babies?"

"Some people have. It just depends. She's not going to ever be well, Claire," he said at last. "She's going to have to be careful, but she's not been given a death sentence, either. There are worse things. With each passing moment we discover more and more about kidney disease. By the time she's a teenager, we may have it conquered totally.''

Claire sighed. She was trying to get him to give her assurances. She knew there weren't any, and she knew he was right. This was a time for joy, not depression. It was just that she was so tired, and they'd been through so much. "I guess I'm being a pain.''

"You're being a mother.''

"Will she be able to come home soon?''

"If everything goes well, she'll be home in a few weeks.''

"That quickly?''

He grinned. Happily. "Claire, she's fine. She's going to be all right.''

"Oh, Jack, I'm so scared.'' When he held out his arms she stepped down from the stool and went to him, needing his strength and support. "I want her to be well.''

"Trust me, Claire,'' he said. "She's all right.''

She drew back. "Are you sure, Jack?''

"I'm positive I'd never lie to you, Claire.''

"Thank you. I'm so glad.'' She'd been afraid to celebrate before. She'd been afraid it wasn't going to last. She leaned her head on his chest again and he held her. "I'm so happy.''

"So am I.'' He took a deep breath that became a sigh of contentment as he pulled her closer and kissed her. "Come on, let's forget the bouillion and hit the sack.''

Claire didn't argue. Without bothering to clean up their mess, Jack led her from the kitchen into the bedroom, flicking off the lights as they went. The lights of the city streaming in the window behind them brightened their way. He had only intended to hold her, but they ended up making love, slowly, gently, as if to comfort rather than excite. It amazed Claire how many ways a man and woman could come together, for this night she felt as though she wasn't sharing sex with him, but that she was giving him a part of her soul, as if their coupling were for the sole purpose of gaining mutual strength and understanding. And yet it was beautiful. They slept curled in each other's arms.

Meghan recovered from surgery quickly. It seemed as if all their problems had occurred before the operation, for she didn't have a bit of trouble with rejection or infection. She got stronger by the day and finally Jack pronounced her fit to leave.

Claire had been preparing for weeks. Although it had actually stopped raining, she swore there was a thundercloud strategically placed over her and she didn't have an umbrella. As spring arrived in Minnesota, she almost wished for winter. The warming trend brought one dreary day of drizzle after another. The rain added to the tons of melting snow that flooded the streets, made the city seem like a sea that had tall buildings popping up here and there. It was wet everywhere. Though it wasn't freezing, it was still cold outside, and the wind whistled through the windows worse than it had in the dead of winter.

On the day Meghan was to leave the hospital, Claire bundled her daughter in the pink jacket, gloves and scarf Jack had given her when they'd first come to Minneapolis.

"You're going to suffocate her," Kathleen remarked as Claire tucked the scarf around Meghan's throat.

"I want her to be warm."

"I'm hot, Mommy."

A nurse standing by laughed. "It's not that cold out, Mrs. Brady."

"It's only fifty degrees out."

"That's warm. And that's a down coat you've put on her. She's not fragile."

Claire glanced at her daughter and couldn't help but laugh, too. Talk about overprotective. She was as bad as Jack had been with her. Meghan looked as though she were going for a visit to the Yukon Territory. She unbundled the scarf. "There, but keep the gloves on."

"Whew, thanks," Meghan said.

Another nurse popped into the room. Claire had planned a dinner at Emilio's as a celebration. Most of the patients turned out to say goodbye, and the hospital staff had been dropping by the room all day long to wish her well. "Take care, now," the nurse said. "Be a good girl."

Meghan gave her a kiss. "I'll come visit."

"Good." The nurse smiled. "We're going to miss you."

"You're going to get tired just kissing everyone," Claire joked when the nurse left, tossing the teddy bear to her daughter to carry. He was literally a mess. "Say, don't you think Soldier's about had it?"

"He's fine, Mommy," Meghan answered. "He's all better, like me."

Claire supposed that "better" depended on your point of view. To her he looked awful. "Maybe we ought to take off some of the Band-Aids."

"His hair comes off. He'll be bald."

"I see." When Claire tried to peel off a Band-Aid, she discovered her daughter was right. "Well, I guess his Band-Aids stay, at least for now."

"They're his scars," Meghan pronounced.

"Oh, well, maybe we can go to Mr. Chin for a transplant," Claire suggested, wondering if the cleaners could re-cover the stuffed animal, "and get rid of some of those scars."

Meghan scoffed at that idea. "You should go to Daddy for a transplant."

"Well, ordinarily that's true, pumpkin," Claire agreed. "But he doesn't do hair well."

"What's this I hear? Casting aspersions on my abilities?" Jack asked, sweeping into the room in a flurried manner, interns and residents on his tail. Unconcerned with propriety, he kissed Claire fully on the lips. Then, picking up Meghan, he kissed her, too, and swung her around before he put her back down. "How are my two favorite girls?"

"We're fine, Daddy." Meghan was charmed by him, as was Claire. The past few weeks, as their child had healed, they'd grown closer than ever. She had a feeling he was going to ask her to marry him at any time and she hoped for his proposal. More than anything she wanted to become his wife again. And she wanted another child with him, too. And another. And another.

"Gosh, you're all bundled up," he said to Meghan.

"Don't," Claire warned. "She's wearing everything I have on her."

"Fine." Jack looked confused. "I hope everyone is hungry. I hear Emilio has fixed lots and lots of food."

"Mommy says we can take it home."

"You could bring it to those of us who have to eat hospital garbage," Kathleen piped up. "Hey, am I gonna get a new roommate, Doc?"

"Probably. Why?"

"I hate getting used to someone new. The kid and I had the television programs all worked out."

"Life's tough all over, Kathy," he told her. Then he patted her foot as '

"Life's tough all over, Kathy," he told her. Then he patted her foot as he always did, teasing her. "Maybe we'll have a Hollywood director for you next time."

Kathleen was going home soon so her worries about a new roommate weren't really too important. Jack had told the teenager the day before that they were sending her back to Ohio. Claire had assumed her parents were having a difficult time financially, and that they had elected to bring her closer to home. After the three months she'd spent with the girl, she only hoped Kathleen's future was as bright as Meghan's. And for all their teasing, the two girls had grown close. They hugged goodbye as Jack took Meghan's suitcase.

The interns and residents scattered in different directions as the three of them headed down the hall—mother, father and child, Meghan's hands tucked in theirs.

"You okay?" Jack asked Claire.

"Yes, I'm fine."

She'd already moved out of Care House, but she felt strange leaving the hospital. She'd spent so much time here she felt as if a part of her life were ending. A bad part of her life. No, she reconsidered: a good part of her life. It was here that a kidney had been found for her daughter and it was here that she had grown to appreciate the man she loved. She'd seen him in his element and understood his concern. Yet, when they walked out the front door she wanted to shout for joy.

After they put Meghan's suitcase in the car they walked to the restaurant. Claire fussed with the scarf again, but Meghan pulled it down so that it was comfortable. "We'll have to get her a spring coat," Jack said.

"All right, I get the message."

He laughed. "We'll all get spring coats."

Claire sidestepped another puddle. "If this rain keeps up, we'll need flippers instead."

"I told you it gets wet here."

"You weren't kidding."

"I like the rain," Meghan said.

"You like the snow, too," Claire remarked. "Don't you have any California spirit in you?"

"Sure," Meghan said, "I got California spirit. I like the sunshine. I like every weather."

Actually, so did Claire. Even the rain, though she joked about it. Since coming back, she'd learned that the rain and snow were fun. Just yesterday she'd gone for a walk in the rain with Jack. They'd skipped through the puddles and let the water stream over their heads. Then they'd gone home and taken a hot shower together and made love.

Right now, though, she just wanted to get to the restaurant without getting her feet wet. It was night, and cold. A freezing wind blew in from the nearby river. She sidestepped a few more puddles. They were almost at Emilio's. When they opened the door and stepped inside, she was amazed. Jack's whole family stood there, waiting.

"Surprise!" they all yelled in unison.

Jack was as astonished as Claire. He stood for a moment, not knowing what to say. "How is everyone?" he finally got out.

Someone laughed. Someone else came to hug Meghan. Another person shook hands with Jack. Pretty soon they were all laughing and talking as usual. Emilio wheeled out a huge cake. He had put on music, and a couple of Jack's sisters started dancing and acting silly. The effect was one of total chaos. Only a few minutes had passed when Jack pushed through the crowd to Claire.

"Look, I'm sorry," he said softly, smiling and nodding at his relatives as they pushed by him, congratulating him on Meghan's homecoming. "I didn't know they were coming. I know you were planning a quiet dinner. I can have everyone leave."

"Why?" she asked, puzzled by his concern. "Everyone's having a good time."

"You don't want them to leave?"

"No."

He shook his head in disbelief. "You've really changed, Claire."

"Yes, I have." She smiled at him and picked up a platter. "Want a piece of garlic bread?"

"I want to kiss you."

"Go ahead."

Jack looked tempted. Instead, he pulled her to her feet and swept her into his arms and started dancing her across the floor in time to the music. "What are you doing?" she asked, shocked by his behavior. True, he kissed her in the hospital, and at home he was quite different, but this was the staid physician in her arms. Jack never danced.

"What I should have done a long time ago," he answered, spinning her around and around the floor. "You know, Claire, the other mistake we made was not having any fun."

"We went tobogganing."

"No, when we were married. And there's nothing as much fun as a real Italian-Irish party." With that he whipped her into the middle of the floor, twirling her faster and faster as his relatives stood in a circle and clapped for them.

That night Claire found out firsthand what a real Italian-Irish party was like, and for the first time she was relaxed enough and confident enough to enjoy it. Jack's family believed in being merry. There was enough food to feed the entire hospital staff, and wine flowed freely. Meghan was the center of attention, and while they lavished it on her, they were very careful not to tax the child. Claire danced until she was ready to drop, and she drank glass after glass of wine. She ate enough garlic bread and spaghetti to add ten pounds to the scales. Even Jack choked when he came near.

"I hear that stuff scares away vampires," he said, fanning his face. "I can see why."

She giggled, pretending to bare her fangs. "I vant to suck your blood."

Although Jack shook his head at her, he seemed amused. "Claire, I think you're drunk."

"I think you're right," she answered, and she hiccuped. "Oops. I'm sorry."

"That's all right. We have reason to celebrate."

"Yes, we do." She laid her head on his shoulder tiredly. "I don't know about you, but I'm ready to go home."

"Let's."

They gathered Meghan and left. The party was still in full swing. Everyone waved and cheered.

"See you Sunday for roast beef," Jack's mother called.

Claire nodded. "We'll be there."

Even though she had fixed up Meghan's bedroom, dusting and changing the sheets, straightening the toys, Claire had forgotten that her daughter had been to Jack's apartment before. She'd spent several summers there. The child was tired when they got home and went directly to her room, having no trouble at all finding it. Jack and Claire both helped her undress and get into her pajamas. Afterward, clutching her teddy bear, Meghan climbed into the frilly pink bed and closed her eyes. "Good night, Mommy," she murmured. "Daddy. It's fun to be home."

"Good night, love," Jack and Claire both answered.

Jack flipped out the light, but they paused in the doorway, both wanting to savor the moment one last time before they closed it for the night. Jack stood behind Claire, holding her. "A nice sight, don't you agree?"

She leaned against him. "Yes. Thank you for giving her back to me," she said softly, gratefully. She had to start realizing just how lucky she was. True, Meghan would never be normal, so to speak, but she was alive and doing well. More than well—she was laughing and skipping and jumping. And more important her little girl was lying in her own bed at home.

"It was my pleasure," Jack answered. "I guess I should give Hal a little credit, though, since he did most of the actual work."

"But you were there."

"I wouldn't have been anywhere else."

She turned to him. "You know, as attached as you get to the kids in your unit, it amazes me that you haven't donated your kidneys ten times over."

"I do get attached to everyone," he admitted. "That's one of the hardest parts of being a doctor."

"Particularly Robbie and Kathleen?"

"Yes." He held her more tightly. "They're very special kids, and you have no idea how I wish I could make them both well. If only I could give them the same thing I've given Meghan—just a chance at life."

"Robbie's still waiting for a kidney," Claire said. "Sybil hasn't said anything, but I think she's giving up hope."

"You can never give up hope," he answered, yet he sighed and led her toward the living room. "Come on, let's go in the other room to talk."

Jack flopped down on the sofa and held out his hand for her. She followed him and curled up beside him. It had become a nightly ritual for them to sit there, staring out at the city beyond. They would talk for hours, never running out of things to say to each other.

This night, Jack seemed to need her. He was quiet at first. Claire always respected his moments of silence. She knew he was thinking, putting things together. He whisked his chin over her head and cuddled her close. "It's beautiful, isn't it?" he said at last, meaning the city.

"Yes, very."

"I'm going to have to have a picture window installed in the bedroom."

"Isn't that a little expensive?"

"Yes, but Meghan's home now. We're going to have to be more careful where we make love, and since I like making love to you here," he went on softly, stroking his hand up her bare arm, "with the lights illuminating your body, we're going to have to make some adjustments."

Just his touch could arouse her. "Children always require adjustments," she answered huskily, but she wasn't thinking of children at all, but rather, the adjustment they could make in the bedroom.

"But worthwhile ones."

"Yes."

He moved his hand to cup her breast, absently twirling his thumb around her nipple. All of a sudden he turned her in his arms and kissed her almost roughly. But she responded, pressing against him eagerly. "Let's go in the bedroom, Claire," he said roughly. "I want you. Now."

Claire wasn't certain what had come over Jack, but she wasn't about to object. They barely got inside the bedroom and closed the door when he pulled her into his arms and kissed her again. His lips were bruising on hers as he pushed her against the wall, his need readily apparent. "I want you, Claire," he repeated. "I want you so badly."

This man in her arms was so unlike the kind, gentle Jack she knew. As if sensing the intensity of his need, and responding with a wild need of her own, she unzipped his pants as he pulled up her dress and pushed aside her underwear. By now they were both gasping, and he lifted her to him, entering her quickly. Even without preamble she was ready for him. She gasped with pleasure as he sank inside her, pausing, hurting so good. Unable to wait, he fumbled with the buttons of her dress. She helped him, releasing her breasts for his mouth. He kissed her nipples, teasing, suckling. She clung to him tightly, choking with need.

He held her close as pleasure rippled through their bodies. Afterward he collapsed his head on her chest. "I love you, Claire."

She clung to his shoulders, trying to stay on her feet. When she could talk, she said, "I know. I love you."

"Did I hurt you? I didn't mean to be so rough. I just seemed to lose control."

"I understand. It was wonderful."

"Are you sure?"

She knew something was wrong. She could sense it. She stroked his dark head. "Is something the matter, Jack?"

"Why?"

"I don't know, you seem . . . preoccupied."

"Did I disappoint you?"

"No."

"I don't want to disappoint you."

"Jack, please tell me what's wrong."

He didn't seem to want to say anything. Finally he sighed. "I just hurt," he said at last. "Sometimes it kills me that I can't do anything for those kids. I didn't mean to take it out on you, but when I touched you I wanted you. I guess I just needed you."

"Oh, Jack." She'd known it was something like that, something that touched his heart. They'd made love so many ways, and it had meant so many things. This was just one more emotion they had shared. "I understand Jack, and I love you."

"I love you, Claire. So damn much it hurts me."

She smiled, pleased by his declaration. "You know what I want to do?" she whispered, still pressed next to him, their bodies touching intimately yet without intimate thoughts.

"What?"

"This may be our last opportunity. We're going to have to watch family fare from now on, and you never have shown me *Frankenstein Meets Wolfman*. I want to put on our pajamas and watch that movie. I want to be scared. With you."

"That's weird, Claire."

"I know. I told you before, I was weird."

"All right," he said, laughing. "You're on. *Frankenstein Meets Wolfman* it is. Right after I kiss you again."

"Yes," Claire agreed, curling her arms around his neck and pressing closer to him, "immediately after you kiss me again."

Chapter 12

For the next several weeks, Claire, Jack and Meghan spent a lot of time together. Jack took his fair share of calls at the hospital and still worked just as hard, but his partnership with Hal Davies was helping to ease his burden and he came home every night. He, Claire and Meghan would do family things like renting videos and watching movies. Claire saw so many happy dogs and thinking cars that she felt certain they were smarter than she was. Once in a while, after Meghan had gone to bed, they'd watch a horror film or a drama. On Jack's days off, they went to every museum in the city of Minneapolis, and to some outside the city. One day Jack even got them plane tickets to Chicago, just to visit the planetarium so Meghan could see the world-renowned star show.

They went to his mother's on Sundays and gave parties of their own. Claire had increasingly learned to appreciate Jack's family, particularly since they were now a family themselves in every sense of the word.

Except for one: Claire and Jack weren't man and wife.

To Claire's chagrin, Jack had yet to ask her to re-marry him. She had waited and hoped, and hoped and waited. Still, three weeks after Meghan's homecoming, he hadn't asked her to do a thing except live with him, and that had been assumed. She was beginning to wonder what was wrong.

His mother felt certain the whole thing was an oversight. "I wish you would let me talk to him," Angeline Brady said to her one Sunday after dinner when they were washing dishes. She had shooed her other daughters and daughters-in-law from the room so that she could speak to Claire alone. "I caused a great deal of your troubles, and it's the least I can do."

"Jack and I caused our own troubles, Mother Brady."

"I know he loves you."

Claire knew that, too. He made it clear day after day.

"I think he's forgotten," Angeline went on.

"That we're not married? Excuse me, I don't mean to be flip, but how do you forget something like that? It is a tad important."

His mother didn't think she was trying to be funny. "You look married, you act married, you may as well be married. You have the same name. He's preoccupied. You know he's busy at the hospital."

"Not that busy. Remember, he's taking time off now. And just last week Father Brady made a point of showing him our old marriage pictures. You can't get much more of a hint than that. Next I'll be sending up smoke signals."

"Then I'll say something to him."

"No, please don't mention it," Claire insisted, not wanting him to ask her because of anything other than wanting to be her husband. "When Jack's ready, he'll ask me."

Angeline snorted her disagreement. "That could be never. You should be married, Claire—if not for your sake, then for Meghan's"

Claire tried to smile. She wanted to be married for *her* sake, not her daughter's, but she was growing as concerned as Angeline about what would happen when Meghan put two and two together. The child was only four years old, but she was bright. Pretty soon it would occur to her that Mommy and Daddy weren't married, either.

Why *hadn't* he asked her?

"So," Jack's mother went on, scrubbing a pot until it gleamed. "What are you going to do?"

"I don't know," Claire answered.

"This is a liberated age. I see ladies walking up to men all the time. They even pay for their own dinners. Why don't *you* ask *him*?"

Somehow those things didn't fit into context. Paying for dinner and asking Jack to marry her seemed to be two different things. "What do you think he'd say?"

Angeline considered for a long moment. "I still say if it's not about medicine, my son is sometimes absent-minded. He's a busy man. He's got his practice and his kidney unit. But he's no fool. If you ask him to marry you, he'll say yes."

Claire wasn't so certain. "Maybe."

"You think about it. In the meantime, I'll give you some roast to take home."

"What will that do?"

Angeline stared at Claire blankly. "Feed you."

Claire laughed and hugged the woman. They'd certainly come a long way in the past few months. "We don't need to be fed, Mother Brady. Jack makes enough money that I could go out to dinner every night and still not be broke. Why don't you give the meat to Mark and Lucy?''

"Good idea. Lucy will make hash out of it.''

Since they were finished, Claire hung up the dish towel. "I'll call you next week and let you know what I decide to do.''

"All right," his mother said. "But don't wait too long.''

"I won't.''

They went into the next room and joined everyone else. The television was playing and as always, his family sat around in groups laughing and chatting happily. Even though the children fought over one toy or another, it didn't seem like chaos to Claire anymore. Jack took her hand when she sat down on the floor near where he was relaxing on the sofa. "Ready to go home?''

She nodded. "Sure.''

"What were you and my mother powwowing about?''

"Nothing. Why?''

"My mother never does dishes with one person unless she's trying to get information or give advice. Which was it?'' He didn't wait for her to answer. Suddenly he frowned at her and lowered his voice to a whisper. "You're not pregnant, are you, Claire?''

What an interesting prospect. Considering her marital status, if that were true, she would certainly have reason for concern. But she was amazed that he would mention such a personal subject in a room full of people, whispered or not, family or not, and she blushed a bright crimson. "No.''

"Oh.'' His face fell. "Well, what's the secret, then?''

"No secret. We just did dishes.''

To his credit Jack didn't probe any further. But the subject wasn't closed. They went home a few minutes later. Once they put Meghan to bed, he took her hand and pulled her toward the bedroom.

"Wait a minute, Jack, I have to hang up our coats." The cleaning lady was coming the next morning, and Claire wanted things straightened up. She scooped up their jackets and headed toward the closet.

"Forget the coats." He kept tugging her toward the bedroom. "Come on."

She frowned at him. "What do you want? I'll only be a minute."

"That's too long."

When he kept insisting she come, she laughed. "What are you doing, Jack?"

He sighed. "Trying to get you into the bedroom so I can make you pregnant."

"Oh." Strangely, she blushed again.

"Don't you want to be pregnant?"

I want to be married! she wanted to shout. "There's no hurry, is there?" she said instead.

He moved close to her. Taking her hand, he placed it on a strategic area of his pants. There was no doubt about his intentions. "I don't mean to shock you, but yes, there is a hurry."

She wasn't a bit shocked. "You're bad, Jack."

"That's not what you say in bed," he whispered huskily into her ear, his breath warm on her neck. She felt her nipples peak as he cupped her breasts and kneaded the areolae with his thumbs.

"I forget what I say." She tossed the jackets aside and slipped her arms around him, pressing close. "I guess I need a reminder."

And what a reminder. Jack made love to her so lustily she wondered where he'd gotten his energy, which didn't seem to wane at all. The next morning he jumped from the bed and hit the shower singing at the top of his lungs.

The man seemed supercharged. Although Claire fixed breakfast, he only had time for coffee and toast. Grabbing his suit coat, he gave her a quick kiss on his way out the door. "I've got surgery all day. Wait dinner for me. We'll watch a video."

"G-rated?"

"R." He waggled his eyebrows at her. "Woman, have I got a deal for you after we put Meghan to bed."

"Another monster movie?"

"Just you wait," he warned.

She laughed and shooed him out the door.

Claire had actually forgotten about marriage or about even considering his mother's suggestion until later in the day, when she happened to pass an old Nash Rambler parked on the street. She had been running to the grocery store to get something for dinner, now regretting not taking the leftover roast. She'd been busy all day, and she needed something to cook. Meghan, more interested in coloring than in going shopping for meat, had stayed at home with the housekeeper.

She almost passed the car when she recognized the make and model. At one time it had been pink, but now the paint was dull and the interior was ripped in places. The thing was about as attractive as the one they'd driven around in four years ago. Not only had Jack made love to her in the back seat, he'd proposed to her there, too. As she stood there staring, her face burned with the memory. So did her body.

Then suddenly an idea began to gel in her mind.

Why not?

She glanced around, hoping the owner might appear. But she was in the middle of a big shopping center at midday. It could take hours for the owner to come back. Searching in her purse for a pen, she scrawled her name and phone number on the back of a blank bank-deposit slip—the only paper she could find—and slipped it under the windshield-wiper blades. Then she hurried into the store, picked up some chicken to broil for dinner and hurried out.

Quickly she drove to the hospital. But after she parked she went the other way, toward Emilio's and the drugstore. All she could do was hope that the apartment they had once lived in wasn't occupied. The last time she'd passed by, it had been dark and empty. She wanted to rent it for the night—one night. She would pick Jack up in the Nash Rambler, drive to the apartment, cook him dinner, and ask him to marry her as they made love on the bed by the red-and-blue neon sign—assuming a bed was still there. And maybe, just maybe, she'd get pregnant in the bargain.

For the next two days Claire felt like the proverbial cat who'd swallowed the canary. She could hardly contain her secret. Jack kept looking at her strangely, as if wondering what was brewing, but she managed to keep quiet. She didn't even breathe a word to Sybil or to Jack's mother. Everything had gone as planned. When he'd called her, the owner of the Nash Rambler had been delighted to rent her the car, as had the owner of the apartment. The man was just as shrewd today as he'd been four years ago, though; she'd had to pay an entire month's rent in advance. Then she'd had to lease furniture, plan a menu and find someone to baby-sit Meghan.

She finally asked Sybil to watch her daughter, but she still didn't say why. Robbie was doing well, though the wait for a kidney was becoming more difficult. Although Sybil was curious, she didn't press for answers to the questions Claire neatly evaded. The only thing left was the meal. Considering her options, Claire decided on something easy: spaghetti, garlic bread and wine. She had to resist the temptation to order it from Emilio. This one night, she wanted to cook for Jack herself.

The morning of the night of her surprise she was nearly beside herself with anxiety, hoping it all would go well. Jack had come home late the night before and they hadn't had much time to talk. She got up with him, making him coffee and toast before he left for the hospital.

"Jack, I was wondering if you were still going to be able to get away tonight," she said as casually as she could manage. Last week she'd asked him to reserve the date on some pretext or other. "Did Hal say he'd take your calls?"

"Yes, he did. Why so nervous?" He came into the room knotting his tie. "Something going on?"

For a moment she thought he might have found out somehow, but then she discounted her suspicion. There was no one who would have told him, because there was no one who knew.

"Nothing's going on. I just thought we might have an evening together," she went on. "Robbie's on spring break so Sybil's offered to watch Meghan for us." Not *quite* a lie—Sybil had offered, after she'd been asked. "I thought we might go to the movies."

"We can watch a movie here."

Why was he being difficult? "Well, we could go somewhere else then."

"Where?"

"Anywhere," she said sharply.

"Are you angry, Claire?" He frowned at her.

"No. No, I'm fine."

"You seemed a little testy."

"Did I? I'm sorry. I'd just kind of like to get out."

"Housewife fever, huh?"

It wasn't like Jack to tease her. She glanced at him, trying to gauge what he was up to. Lately he'd been acting oddly too. "Yes," she said. "I guess so."

"Okay." He was readily agreeable. "Sounds like fun."

"Are you sure you're off?"

"I'm sure. I'll even remind Hal later."

Since he came up behind her and she turned around and slipped her arms around his neck. "Are you sure it's no problem?"

"This means a lot to you, doesn't it, Claire?" he asked with another frown. "What's going on?"

But it wasn't quite a concerned frown, and once again Claire couldn't help but wonder if he'd guessed her surprise. "Nothing," she repeated, studying him closely. "It's just a night out. You've been slipping back into your old habits lately and I want to make sure you can get away."

"Last night was an emergency. I'm sorry." Now his frown did seem serious.

"Jack, you don't have to apologize for your work. I understand."

"Are you sure? I don't want you to be upset."

"I'm not upset."

"Yes, you are. I can tell."

"Jack, I am not upset." It was silly, but she was getting upset now. "Never mind. Let's just forget it. Believe me, this is not worth getting into an argument over."

"No? Then why are we arguing?" He held her by the shoulders. "You are testy, but don't worry, I'll be there. What time?"

"Five."

"Where?"

"Here."

He kissed her and grabbed his suit coat as he went out the door. "I'm late, I've got to go. I'll see you later. Like clockwork."

"Sure. Like clockwork."

"I love you."

"Right." She laughed.

"I'll be here, Claire!"

She waved as he left. Then she started clearing away their coffee cups. For weeks they hadn't argued at all and she'd almost blown that record on a silly dinner. But Jack was right: the evening did mean a lot to her. A sense of excitement made her want to waltz around the house as she got ready. She had an interesting day as well as an interesting evening ahead of her.

She had to think of ways to pop the question. Would she go down on her knees? Or ask in between kisses?

Jack grinned as he got into his car to drive to the hospital. Claire thought she was surprising him, but he had a surprise of his own in store. He'd actually known about her plans for days. Always the shrewd businessman, the owner of the apartment building had called Jack at the hospital and asked him if he wanted to sign a long-term lease on the apartment. Jack had also found out about the car when the owner called the one night he was home to confirm the date. After that, it wasn't hard to figure out what she was up to. She was hardly subtle. She'd been walking around grinning for a week. The night his father had shown him their marriage certificate, he'd wanted to laugh, knowing that the only reason he hadn't asked her yet was because he was waiting for her mother to find their original wedding ring.

Truthfully, at first he'd forgotten they weren't married. They loved each other, and that was what mattered. They were happy, they were a family.

Then one day he'd glanced at her hand and remembered. It had seemed so naked, but a slim gold band would fix that. Later that night he'd called Annabelle Warren, asking her to search for the ring and bring it to Minneapolis as a surprise.

So far she was still searching, but tonight he had decided to give Claire another ring, whether or not her mother found theirs. Surprises were great, but he loved Claire desperately and wanted to make her his wife. If he had to wait for a ring, this delay might go on forever. When he'd thought she was pregnant, he'd been happy and yet angry at himself at the same time. It made him realize that there was no reason to wait one more day. They could go to city hall tomorrow, unless she wanted a bigger wedding.

Jack paused abruptly. He'd pulled into a parking space in the hospital lot and opened his door to get out. Would Claire want a wedding? he wondered. They'd had a hurried affair before—a few words in front of a magistrate, followed by a night of lovemaking. Maybe this time they should do it right. He had to remember that as much as he loved her, as much as he loved to *make love* to her, he had to hold back and not make her think that sex was the only thing between them. That's what she'd thought last time, even though she'd meant the world to him. The day he'd come home from the hospital to find her gone, he'd nearly gone out of his mind.

"Having car trouble, Jack?" Hal Davies asked, getting out of his own car.

Jack glanced at his new partner. "No. Everything's fine. Just thinking."

"About that pretty wife of yours, I'll bet."

Jack smiled. "That obvious, huh?"

"We should all be so happy. Say, I wanted to talk to you about the Miller boy. I've done some tests on him and I wanted you to take a look at the chart."

"Something wrong?"

"I'm not sure what's going on. That's why I'd appreciate your opinion."

Jack didn't have a chance to consider whether or not Claire wanted a wedding anymore that morning. He went into the hospital discussing a case with Hal. After that he had several surgeries in a row and then a consultation at Parkside. Later on, when he could get the operating room again, he had to insert a shunt in one of the kidney patients. All he knew was that he wasn't about to disappoint her for any reason. He would be home on time tonight if it killed him.

Claire spent most of her day pampering herself, getting ready for her big evening. After she played with Meghan for a while she took a long, leisurely bath and shampooed her hair, brushing it until her scalp hurt. The car had been delivered early that morning, but she still had to go to the apartment and cook dinner. Then she had to get back home in time for Jack's arrival. The surprise was growing so complicated, she was almost wishing she'd just blurted out her proposal and gotten it over with.

But she knew it would be worth it when she saw the look on his face. At about three o'clock she bundled Meghan up and headed for Sybil's. "Just tell anyone who calls I've left with Meghan. Okay?'' she told the house-keeper.

"Sure," the woman agreed. "Are you expecting any-one to call?"

"Just my mother or maybe Jack. I don't want him to come home until I'm back, though, so be sure and give him the message if he calls."

"Yes, ma'am," the housekeeper answered.

Since it was mid-April, spring was in full bloom. On the way over to Sybil's, Meghan pointed out all the flowers growing so rampantly. She was especially fasci-nated with the tulips. They had to be force-bloomed in California, and the child had never seen one before. "Look, Mommy, a purple one."

"It's lovely." Claire smiled at her daughter. Life was so fascinating to Meghan. Each moment brought a bright, new discovery. Looking at her now, it was hard to believe how sick she'd been four months ago.

"Does Auntie Sybil have tulips?"

"I don't know. They just recently bloomed. Robbie's going to be home today. You'll get to play with him."

"When's Robbie gonna get a kidney?"

"I don't know that, either," Claire answered. "I hope soon."

"I like my kidney."

From out of the mouths of babes . . . Claire laughed. "I'll bet you do. I like your kidney, too," she teased.

"How can you like it, Mommy? You can't see it."

"Oh, but I see the results!" Claire wrinkled her nose at her daughter as she pulled her car up in front of Sy-bil's apartment and parked. "Well, we're here."

They walked up the steps hand in hand. Since it was April, and warm, Claire had let Meghan discard her huge jacket for a lighter coat.

Sybil opened the door for them right away, beaming welcome. "Well, look who's here. Come on in." She glanced at Claire. "Got a minute to gossip?"

She hadn't, but since Sybil had been such a good friend, she felt obligated to talk for a little while. "Sure."

As Meghan went to find Robbie, Claire walked into the apartment. Sybil gave a sniff as Claire went by. "Wow. That's really some kind of perfume. Did you say you were going to a movie tonight? Smells more like a seduction scene coming up."

Claire flushed. "It's that obvious?"

"It is a seduction scene?"

"Never mind. You're too anxious to know." Claire glanced into the other room. "How's Robbie?"

"Doing great, actually. I'm the one who's down. He loves school here, you know. I can't stand it. He likes the big city, going to high school. He's a hotshot. He's always with the girls. They're hanging on his arms, they think he's so cute. Back in Montana there were maybe three girls for every fifty boys. What can you expect?"

"Love?"

"I hope not. Frankly, though, if he does get a kidney, I don't know if he's going to want to go home."

"Would you make him?"

"Are you kidding? I told you once, I'd do anything for that kid. Even live here."

"It's not so bad," Claire said.

"Oh, yeah? You left once."

Claire shrugged. "I was young and foolish. Minnesota's a great place to live."

"Love," Sybil repeated. "Look what it does to you." She shook her head in disbelief and then she laughed and went on talking. "Actually, anywhere is a good place to live, as long as you're happy with someone. I'm thinking of going ahead and selling the ranch. I could use the money, and what the hell have I got there, anyhow? Ira's dead.''

"Your way of life?"

"So I don't rope cows anymore. My way of life can be changed. You're proof of that. Are you happy, Claire?''

"Very."

"I'm glad. You know I was always pulling for you."

"I know. Well—" Claire stood up "I should get going. I've got a few things to do before this evening."

"I'll bet. Wish I were a mouse in the corner."

Claire grinned. "I'm glad you're not. I'd be inhibited. We'll probably pick up Meghan around ten or eleven. Is that too late?"

"Not for me. See you then. Sure you don't want me to keep her overnight?"

Claire paused, considering. It would be nice to be able to spend the night with Jack. "Would that be a problem?"

"Not at all. And you know she'd love it, as close as she and Robbie became in the hospital. She can wear one of my T-shirts to sleep in."

"All right. Fine. We'll pick her up in the morning. If you do need to get hold of me—for any reason at all—" she said, feeling a little twinge of guilt, "Jack will no doubt have his pager."

"Sure thing. Don't worry about her; she'll be fine."

Meghan was thrilled to stay overnight. Claire kissed her daughter and left. She was already running late. She'd have to hurry to get everything fixed.

Even though it was spring, the apartment was cold. Claire had begun to think her problems with the weather had been strictly related to where they had lived. The walls seemed unnaturally damp, perhaps because the place was so sparsely furnished. The only things she'd rented were a table, two chairs and a bed, and if that wasn't a message, she really would need to send up smoke signals. She'd bought candles and flowers to set around, and she'd already stowed the groceries in the refrigerator. All she had to do later was heat up the sauce, cook the noodles and bake the garlic bread. She'd come to put the sheets on the bed. She'd finally decided to be wicked and had bought a set in red satin. They weren't totally impractical, she told herself; they'd match the bedroom at home, too.

Home.

She paused, realizing she had truly come home. Sybil was right. A person could live anywhere, as long as there was someone they cared about there. If only she'd realized that before—she could have saved both herself and Jack a great deal of pain.

She glanced at her watch. It was close to five o'clock. if she didn't hurry, she was going to miss Jack. Quickly she made the bed and sprinkled perfume over the sheets. He'd love the smell.

It was almost five exactly when she left the apartment. She nodded to a couple of nurses she recognized coming from the emergency room, apparently heading home. "Mrs. Brady," one of them spoke. "How've you been?"

Claire smiled. "Great."

They both walked on. Then suddenly, one of them turned back. "Mrs. Brady, did you hear about Kathleen?"

"Kathy from the unit?" Claire paused.

"Yes, she's in surgery."

"Here? Now?" Claire was astonished.

The nurse nodded. "Dr. Brady's operating on her."

"I thought she went home." Claire was worried. "What happened?"

"She was discharged," the nurse confirmed. "Her parents came to pick her up today, but they got in an automobile accident on the way out of the city. It was pretty bad. A truck jumped the median and hit them broadside. She ruptured her spleen and lacerated her kidney and her arm got slashed from the glass shards. I think it messed up her fistula. She was bleeding heavily when we sent her up to surgery."

"What are they going to do?"

"They're going to have to remove her kidney in order to stop the bleeding. I don't know what they're going to do if they have to dialyze her; fix the fistula probably. They called Dr. Brady from a consultation at Parkside to operate on her. Dr. Davies is there, too. I thought you'd like to know."

"Oh, yes, thank you." Claire had spent so much time with Kathy, the teenager was like her own child. Jack loved her, too. She couldn't help but remember the night he'd been so upset over both Kathy and Robbie. And Kathy had had so many complications that an operation was the last thing she needed to go through.

"I'm surprised Dr. Brady didn't call you," the nurse went on speaking.

"Yes, so am I, but I haven't been home. Will that mess up her chances for a transplant?"

"No, the kidney wasn't functioning, anyway. It just has to be removed. But it's an operation."

When the nurses left, Claire glanced at her watch for the third time in less than fifteen minutes. Obviously Jack wasn't going to make it for dinner, but that didn't upset her. Right then, her plans for the evening seemed unimportant. Strange how something like this could put things in perspective. At the moment the important thing was that the life of a child—a child she loved—was in Jack's hands. She hesitated only a moment. Then she hurried across the street toward the hospital. She wanted to be there not only for Kathleen, but for Jack. For if anything happened to the girl, she knew he would be devastated. And so would she.

Chapter 13

The operating room was cold, as usual, but Jack knew as soon as he started surgery that he would begin to sweat under the bright lights. As he donned his sterile gown and gloves, he glanced at the young girl lying on the table, so quiet and still. Kathleen had already been put to sleep and was ready to be operated on. The surgery would be difficult, delicate, and the clock on the wall told him they didn't have much time to fool around.

It also told him he'd missed Claire's surprise.

"Did anyone get in touch with my wife?" he asked the nurse who snapped first one glove and then the other on his hands.

"I talked to your housekeeper," the green-clad woman answered from behind her mask. "She said your wife left with your daughter."

"Did she know I was going to be late?"

"I don't think so, Dr. Brady. I think she was gone already."

"But you're not sure?"

"No."

"Got a family problem, Jack?" Hal Davies came into the room right then, holding his scrubbed hands erect for a towel. "If you need to go, I can manage the operation by myself."

Jack glanced again at Kathleen. In the months he'd cared for her, she'd become as important to him as his own child. "No, I'll stay."

"Sure?"

Jack hoped to hell Claire understood. A patient was close to dying and he had to stay. If this night hadn't meant so much to her, he wouldn't have been at all worried. But she'd fussed about it for days, prepared for it. Would the disappointment of his not showing up create a rift in their relationship?

"Any way someone can go across the street and check to see if she's at our old apartment? I think she might have gone there for the night."

"I'm sorry, Dr. Brady," the nurse answered. "I'd like to help, but we're awfully busy. We're shorthanded and all that's here is the on-call staff. Next door they're operating on the guy that hit this kid and we've got an emergency appendectomy next. I don't have anyone to spare."

Jack nodded. "Never mind. I'll find her later. If she does happen to call, please tell her I've had an emergency."

"Will do. If I get a chance I'll try to call her again." The nurse smiled. He could see her eyes shine from behind the mask. "You've been awfully relaxed lately, and I wouldn't want you going back to your old ways."

"Neither would my wife," he muttered.

Only she wasn't his wife. Not yet, anyhow.

"Oh, by the way," the nurse went on. "You did get a call earlier from a Mrs. Annabelle Warren. You were at Parkside and I forgot to give you the message. She's coming in on the eight o'clock flight. Said she'd take a taxi over to your house."

Now he had his ex-mother-in-law coming to town and he didn't know where Claire had gone. All he could do was hope that she loved him enough to not be upset that he was standing her up on a very important night of their lives.

Stepping up to the operating table, he picked up a scalpel and glanced at the team standing by. "Let's get going," he said.

Claire had never met Kathleen's parents, and although she'd seen pictures of them, she didn't feel comfortable going up to them in the midst of their grief and introducing herself. Had they been alone it would have been one thing, but they had each other. They were older, perhaps in their fifties or sixties. The woman kept crying and the man kept comforting her, patting her on the back and offering encouragement.

How encouraging could it be to know that your daughter was in surgery, fighting for her life? To know that she was already sick and that now she might die from something totally unrelated?

Claire had gone to the operating-room desk to leave a message for Jack, but no one had been there. She supposed they were short staffed, which was typical on nights and weekends. She had every intention of waiting, though. She'd been around this place long enough to know that when he was done, Jack would come through the double doors and speak to the family. She would stay

in the background and wait for him. All she wanted was
to be here for him in case something went wrong.

Poor Kathleen. She couldn't imagine the teenage girl
in surgery. All she could see was her perched in the bed,
snapping her gum and making wisecracks. The last time
they'd talked, Claire had teased her about an intern she'd
become infatuated with.

Now she waited for what seemed hours—actually, for
what *was* hours. She had almost given up when Jack
came out. He came through the doors still dressed in his
green scrubs. Sweat dampened his chest and cap and he
looked tired, very tired, and upset about something.
Claire stayed in the background until he was done talking with Kathleen's family. She could imagine what the
parents were feeling. She could tell from their reactions
that the girl had made it through surgery. She didn't
know the prognosis, though, and when Jack turned
away, she stepped toward him.

"Hi," she said shyly, smiling. "How's Kathy?"

He stood stock-still. "Claire?"

"You look surprised."

"I am. What the hell are you doing here?" He'd just
spent the last fifteen minutes on the phone himself, trying
to track her down.

She was taken aback by his sharp tone. "I've been
here."

"All evening?"

She couldn't understand why he was so angry, but it
was clear that he was furious—but at her? "Most of it,"
she said. "I came over as soon as I heard."

"Where's Meghan?"

"With Sybil."

"I thought you had left with her," he accused angrily.
"I got a message that you'd left."

"That was this afternoon. Jack, we're not communicating here," she said, growing more and more puzzled by his behavior. "Something's going wrong."

"I have been trying to get in touch with you, Claire. That's what's going wrong. And I didn't have time to fool around doing it, either. I thought you were upset because I didn't make it to dinner."

"Wait a minute." All of a sudden it became clear to her to what he was alluding. "You thought I left you because you didn't make it home tonight?"

"I didn't know what to think."

She frowned at him. "That's even worse. After all we've been through together, what we've meant to each other, I can't believe you could think that of me. How shallow do you think I am?"

"I don't think you're at all shallow." He reached to touch her hand. "I'm sorry—"

"No, wait a minute." Now she was angry. "You were willing to believe I had left you? You *actually* believed that, Jack? I wanted to ask you to *marry* me. I made plans."

"I know. That's why I was so upset. I didn't want to disappoint you."

"You know what, Jack?" She was terribly hurt. "That disappoints me more than anything." For the first time since she'd come here she was really furious, down-deep furious. The fact that he could doubt her at all cut deeply. She snatched up her purse and started to walk away.

But he didn't let her leave. He grabbed her arm and pulled her back. "Claire, this is silly. Wait a minute. We're both overreacting. I saw you and I was surprised. I thought you'd gone, but I was wrong. Why can't we leave it at that?"

"Because we can't. You don't trust me."

Jack glanced around, realizing that half the hospital, including Kathleen's parents, was standing about, listening. Claire glanced around and blushed.

"Come on." He tugged at her hand. "We need to talk."

"Don't you think we've talked enough for one night?"

"No, I don't. All we've done is argue. Senselessly." He pulled her into a room and closed the door behind them. It was the men's locker room and he sat her on the bench and stood in front of her, holding her by her arms. "Look, I know we're not out of the woods yet, you and I. There are a lot of adjustments we have to make. We haven't even talked about our future, what we want together, if we're going to make it together." He took a deep breath. "Hell, I'd like to throw you down on the floor and make love to you and forget all this talk, but that was our problem before. We never talked. We've got to get some things clear between us."

"I'm sorry, Jack, I guess I'm not following you. What is it you want to get clear?"

"Don't you understand why I'm angry? Don't you understand that it's not you I don't trust? It's me. I was more concerned tonight about you than about Kathleen. I had to operate on that kid, who means a hell of a lot to me, and yet all I thought about was you. Do you know how that makes me feel? What kind of doctor that makes me?"

It had never occurred to Claire that he would doubt himself. "Oh, Jack, I'm sorry."

"So am I."

In fact, he looked destroyed by it. But Claire had to reach him with logic. "Jack, look, this was a fluke. I'm sorry we argued. It was all caused by a misunderstanding. You thought I was somewhere and I thought—"

"No, Claire," he cut in almost sadly. "It wasn't a misunderstanding. It was based on our relationship. You see, I love you so much, I'd be willing to do anything to keep you, and that includes having you in the operating room with me, looking at the clock and wondering if you're upset or if you're going to leave me, what you're doing or where you're at."

He sounded so serious, so final. "What do you want to do about it?"

"I don't know."

She licked her lips nervously, afraid to ask, afraid of his answer. "Do you—Jack," she whispered, "do you want me to leave?"

"Oh, God, no," he said, taking her hands in his and holding on tight. His voice was as hoarse as hers. "God, Claire, I love you."

"But if I'm interfering in your work—" It hurt her as much as him, and she could tell he was torn up inside. "Jack, I don't want to be an obsession with you. I don't want to be in the operating room with your patients. I just want to be here for you, waiting for you to come home. I want to be your wife."

"I don't know if the two are compatible, Claire. I don't know where we go from here."

"We've been through so much." For once in her life she was willing to beg. "I don't want to lose you. I love you."

"I love you, Claire."

"Then what's the problem?"

"I don't think love's enough."

"That was Kathleen on the table, Jack."

"But what if it hadn't been Kathleen? What if it had been someone you didn't know?"

"It would be the same thing, because it would be someone you care about."

"Dr. Brady?" After knocking, a nurse stuck her head in the door. "We just got a call from United Network. They've got a kidney for Robbie Parker. It's in St. Paul. Do you want me to get in touch with his mother? Or do you want Dr. Davies to handle it? He's on call."

Jack glanced at Claire. She could see the indecision in his face. He was tired, he'd been on his feet all day, but Robbie was his patient. Yet there was Claire.

She placed her hand on his arm. "Jack, I know you have a patient, so I'll only keep you another minute. There are a couple of things I still need to say."

She drew a deep breath before she began. This was probably the most important speech of her life. She just hoped she said the right things. Their relationship depended on it. Did she love him enough to leave him? "Jack, we can either break this off or we can try to make it work. So far it's gone pretty well. And I'm not sure what happened tonight to make it go wrong. Maybe it's the full moon or our biorhythms or something crazy, but I didn't know you were unhappy. I didn't know I was becoming a burden."

"Claire, I didn't mean that you're a burden."

"Wait," she said. "Let me finish. I'd like you to know that I'd be glad to wait for you, even if it takes all night. That spaghetti dinner I fixed isn't even important."

"But it is, don't you see?"

"Please let me finish," she said, trying to hold back tears. She had to make him see they weren't at an impasse. "I—I also want you to know that if we can put this together, I won't ever leave, even if it's in the middle of a blizzard, even if it's in the middle of a tornado or even if you don't come home for ten days or a month or a year. I've grown, Jack. I've grown up. And I know that if you love someone you're willing to give as well as take. I was a taker before. I was selfish. But if you want me to leave, I will." Now the tears did start to slide down her cheeks—silent tears, the worst kind, because they ached inside. "You see, I love you," she went on. "And I don't want to take your strength as a doctor away. You're special. So special, Jack."

He clutched her in a tight embrace. "What are we going to do?"

She sniffled. "Operate on Robbie Parker?"

He paused for a long moment. "You'll wait? You're sure?"

"Isn't that what doctors' wives always do?"

He buried his head in the curve of her neck. "Lord, how I love you."

She held him, running her fingers through his dark hair. "I love you, Jack."

"Dr. Brady?"

He glanced toward the nurse. "I'll be right there." Then he looked back at Claire. "Look, I should tell you, your mother's coming here tonight. She's on the eight o'clock flight from Los Angeles."

"My moth—"

"Wait." He held up his hand, now asking her for time. "She's bringing your wedding band. I wanted to have it before I asked you to marry me again. I wanted to give it to you all over again, and tell you that I wasn't going to make the same mistakes as before."

"They aren't the same mistakes. They're new ones."

He laughed, as she'd intended. "Can we talk more later?"

"I think we have to."

"Think we can salvage our marriage?"

She smiled at him. "I think we have to."

"Dr. Brady?" the nurse said again.

Jack stood up, reluctant to let go of Claire's hand. He didn't ever want her to get away from him. "Robbie's got a beeper, hasn't he?" Most transplant patients waiting for surgery carried one so they could be contacted immediately.

"I believe so," the nurse answered.

"Then get his mother on the phone. Tell Dr. Davies to go for the kidney. I'll get ready to scrub."

She watched him go. For an evening that had started out so joyously, it had certainly turned out rottenly. Then again, maybe there would be some joy.

This time Claire waited with Sybil while they operated on Robbie. Meghan slept peacefully on the sofa in the corner, covered by a blanket an aide had brought. The two women didn't say much—there wasn't much to talk about. Claire recalled how they assumed nearly the same positions when they had been waiting for Meghan. She took up her vigil at the window, and Sybil sat in a chair by the door. The operation took several hours, and it was well past midnight when Jack came back out of the operating room. He pulled off his cap and ran his hand wearily through his hair. If Claire had thought him tired before, it didn't compare to now.

But he smiled at Sybil. "Well, we did it. Better put that ranch up for sale and find a house by the local high school."

Sybil had mentioned Robbie's preference for Minneapolis to Jack, too. "Thank goodness," the woman said, letting her breath out all at once. She hugged Jack. "Thank you."

Claire felt as if all she'd done this night was cry. She felt tears start to slip down her cheeks again. She was so happy for her friend.

"We're going to put him in Intensive Care tonight," Jack went on telling the woman. "He's fine, but we don't have the staff to recover him properly. He'll go to a room in the kidney unit tomorrow."

"Thank you," Sybil said again. She was weeping openly now. "Thank you so much."

Jack patted her on the shoulder. "Thank all the latest technology," he told her. "I didn't have a heck of a lot to do with it."

Sybil laughed. "Oh, sure. You expect me to believe that? Dr. Brady, there's not much I can do for you, but if you ever need a cow, just let me know."

He laughed outright then. "I don't need a cow, but I could sure use a good night's sleep." He glanced at Claire. "I'll be ready to go in a few minutes. I need to change clothes."

"I'll wake Meghan."

"Don't bother. I'll carry her."

"You going to be able to work it out?" Sybil asked Claire when Jack left the room.

"How did you know we were having a problem?"

"When I went to the washroom before, I heard a couple of the operating room nurses talking."

Claire blushed. Gossip was certainly rampant in this place.

"Go on. I'll watch Meghan a few minutes. How long can it take when two people love each other?"

Thank goodness Jack was alone in the dressing room. Taking a deep breath, she pushed open the door and went inside. "Jack? Where are you?"

"I'm almost ready." He came around the corner buttoning his shirt. He had draped his tie around his neck and he carried his suit jacket.

"Are you too tired to talk now?"

"Do you want to talk now?"

"Yes. I don't want to go another minute with this rift between us."

"There's no rift, Claire." Moving close, he pushed a stray lock of hair from her face.

"Just a giant chasm, then?" she joked weakly. "About the size of the Grand Canyon?" She swallowed hard, trying not to let her emotions get the better of her. She couldn't cry again—she would flood the place. But it meant so much to her. *He* meant so much to her. "Jack, I couldn't stand it if we couldn't work this out."

"I think it's already worked out." He stroked his hand along her cheek and leaned down to kiss her.

"No, it isn't. Wait, Jack," she told him, drawing back. "You were right before. We can't solve our problems with kisses and making love all the time. That was the mistake we made the first time. Have you—have you come to a conclusion yet?"

"About what?"

"My leaving."

He shook his head. "You can't leave, Claire," he said softly, "because I would never let you go. I didn't want you there, but you were with me the last time I was in the operating room."

"Just now? With Robbie?" What was he getting at?

"Yes, with Robbie." His voice was still soft, rueful. "But I figured since you were there I'd take advantage of you, and I decided that if you ever left me, I'd go to the ends of the earth to get you back. It didn't matter. I had to have you. And if that's an obsession, so be it. You see,

Claire—'' he stepped closer, cupping her cheek with his hand ''—you're my life and my love, and I discovered that you're always with me, one way or another, and I was looking at the clock because I *wanted* to look at the clock. I wanted to be with you and that's all right. There's nothing wrong with it, because I still did a good job. I can be a good doctor and good husband, too, as long as you're willing to put up with me.''

She was so choked up there wasn't much she could get out. ''Jack, I love you.''

That was all that was necessary. He swept her into his arms and crushed her next to his body. ''I love you, too. Think you can put up with me?''

''Oh, yes.''

''Just remind me if I get out of line, okay?''

''Yes.''

''Let's go home.''

''My mother!'' All of a sudden Claire remembered her mother. In all the confusion, the operations and crises, she'd forgotten her own mother.

Jack grinned. ''Don't worry. This is one time my family's come in handy. I somehow found a free person who could call and have my brother pick her up. I just got a message a few minutes ago that they arrived at my mom's. We're supposed to go for roast tomorrow.''

Claire's heart sang with joy. ''Thank you, Jack.''

''Let's go get Meghan,'' he said, equally joyful. ''And go home.''

Home. It sounded so wonderful.

''Now,'' he went on as they went out the door to the locker room and headed toward the waiting room and their daughter, "the way I see it, the only thing we have left to decide is how we want to be married."

"What do you mean, how?"

"Do you want a big wedding? Or do you want to elope again? I can tell you one thing: whatever you choose, it had better be fast. I don't intend to wait very long to get my ring on your finger. This wait nearly cost me dearly."

"I want to go to the magistrate tomorrow," she said, "and spend tomorrow night in our old apartment."

"You're on," he answered. They walked into the room and Jack picked up their daughter from the sofa. "Thanks," he said to Sybil.

Claire gave the woman a hug. "We'll be here in the morning to see how Robbie is."

"He's going to be fine," she said confidently. "Never give up hope."

How true. Claire hugged her friend again. "Yes, never give up hope."

They went down the hall and to the elevator. Claire walked alongside Jack and Meghan. When they got outside the hospital she looked up and there was the North Star in the sky—constant. As she paused, her eye was caught by a piece of red lying on the ground in the midst of some tulips.

Her scarf.

"Wait a minute." She walked to where it fluttered in the wind and picked it up. The hospital had recently planted some trees. A small maple grew in the corner, a tiny sapling barely clinging to life, and she tied the scarf around it.

"What's that for?" Jack asked.

"Hope." She walked back to the sidewalk and took his hand, squeezing tightly. "Success. And us."

"Us." He squeezed back. They walked on into the night and to the joy of finding each other at last.

* * * * *

Keepsake

1989
IS THE YEAR
OF THE MAN!

What makes a romance? A special man, of course, and Silhouette Desire celebrates that fact with *twelve* of them! From Mr. January to Mr. December, every month spotlights the Silhouette Desire hero—our **MAN OF THE MONTH**.

Sexy, macho, charming, irritating…irresistible! Nothing can stop these men from sweeping you away. Created by some of your favorite authors, each man is custom-made for pleasure—*reading* pleasure—so don't miss a single one.

Diana Palmer kicks off the new year, and you can look forward to magnificent men from **Joan Hohl**, **Jennifer Greene** and many, many more. So get out there and find your man!

MAN OF THE MONTH…

MAND-1

ATTRACTIVE, SPACE SAVING BOOK RACK

Display your most prized novels on this handsome and sturdy book rack. The hand-rubbed walnut finish will blend into your library decor with quiet elegance, providing a practical organizer for your favorite hard-or soft-covered books.

Only $9.95

Approximately 16" x 8" when assembled

Assembles in seconds!

To order, rush your name, address and zip code, along with a check or money order for $10.70* ($9.95 plus 75¢ postage and handling) payable to *Silhouette Books*.

Silhouette Books
Book Rack Offer
901 Fuhrmann Blvd.
P.O. Box 1396
Buffalo, NY 14269-1396

Offer not available in Canada.

BKR-2A

*New York and Iowa residents add appropriate sales tax.